Books by Alexa Milne

The Call of Home

Choosing Home
Returning Home
Staying Home

Lust Bites

Stay

Single Titles

Sporting Chance
Not Every Time
Comfort Zone
A Bell Rings

I0570499

Staying Home

ISBN # 978-1-78686-076-7

©Copyright Alexa Milne 2016

Cover Art by Posh Gosh ©Copyright 2016

Interior text design by Claire Siemaszkiewicz

Pride Publishing

This is a work of fiction. All characters, places and events are from the author's imagination and should not be confused with fact. Any resemblance to persons, living or dead, events or places is purely coincidental.

All rights reserved. No part of this publication may be reproduced in any material form, whether by printing, photocopying, scanning or otherwise without the written permission of the publisher, Pride Publishing.

Applications should be addressed in the first instance, in writing, to Pride Publishing. Unauthorised or restricted acts in relation to this publication may result in civil proceedings and/or criminal prosecution.

The author and illustrator have asserted their respective rights under the Copyright Designs and Patents Acts 1988 (as amended) to be identified as the author of this book and illustrator of the artwork.

Published in 2016 by Pride Publishing, Newland House, The Point, Weaver Road, Lincoln, LN6 3QN, United Kingdom.

No part of this book may be reproduced, scanned, or distributed in any printed or electronic form without permission. Please do not participate in or encourage piracy of copyrighted materials in violation of the authors' rights. Purchase only authorised copies.

Pride Publishing is a subsidiary of Totally Entwined Group Limited.

If you purchased this book without a cover you should be aware that this book is stolen property. It was reported as "unsold and destroyed" to the publisher and neither the author nor the publisher has received any payment for this "stripped book".

The Call of Home

STAYING HOME

ALEXA MILNE

Dedication

Thanks as always go to Dawn and Faith and also to Avylinn for reading this through for me. This story is also for my family who stayed at home in South Wales while I moved away. But most of all, it is for Cath for taking care of me while I was definitely staying home through injury. Lastly, I'd like to thank all those people whose experiences helped with research for this book.

Chapter One

"What the hell is the matter with you today? Mel will be coming down the aisle in ten minutes and you're away with the fairies."

Sam shook himself. "I'm sorry. I didn't sleep well last night. Probably the thought of marrying my little brother to his lovely bride."

"I'm supposed to be the nervous one, not you," Gus protested. "You've been acting funny for weeks now. It's not the end of the world, splitting up with Emily. If I can find someone, you can. Perhaps you should consider shaving the beard."

Hearing the concern in his brother's voice, Sam stroked his face nervously. He glanced toward the back of the kirk again, taking in the whitewashed walls, bereft of decoration as befitted a Protestant church. He shouldn't have these feelings. Brodie as still mourning his husband. The pain still clear on his face every time he mentioned Harry's name. In his heart, which ached every time he saw him, Sam wanted to offer comfort, but he had no right to want to touch him, to hold him, to take him in his arms and tell him everything would be fine. Listening, caring, ministering to one of his flock—those were his tasks. And he was straight—except he wasn't—and the one man who knew that also sat in his church, the best friend of the man who filled his dreams, day and night. Sam wondered what Brodie and Darach were talking about, the pair of them sitting so close to each other on the wooden seats. Darach McNaughton glanced up and caught his gaze. Heat flushed his cheeks, and he shifted his attention to the woman who had set foot in the church as the music started.

"Showtime," he whispered to Gus. "Mel makes a stunning bride. You're a lucky man." He waited as Mel proceeded slowly up the aisle on her father's arm until his brother, and his bride, stood side by side.

"Dearly beloved, we are gathered here to witness..."

The weather stayed fair for the photographs. Even in June, there was no guarantee of sunshine in Scotland. Sam stood among his family, together, but separate as always. Maybe it was being the lone blond among his redheaded brothers that set him apart. His mother used to call him her special one, being the one who had inherited her coloring. She'd sat in the front row next to his father. On the other side sat his grandmother, Sarah, his remaining grandparent, now in her late eighties but still as strong-minded as she'd ever been.

They made an impressive group in the photographs, he and his four brothers. Alec, the eldest, age thirty-five, named after his father, now married with three children and inheritor of their parents' butcher shop. Next came Stuart, two years older than himself, also married and father of twin girls, a car mechanic who owned his own garage. Sam stood taller than his elder brothers, and, unlike them in their kilts, he wore his clerical uniform. Next came Hamish, a teacher, the brother who had left the area. Lastly, there was Angus, or Gus as everyone knew him, who sat at the front next to his beautiful bride, a smile as wide as the Moray Firth and as glorious as the sun shining above them. How Sam envied him and his brothers, so certain about themselves and their choices, while he floundered, unable to face who he was, or what he was. He smiled when required and agreed how handsome everyone looked, happy when the photographer had finished and he could stay on the sidelines once more, thankful his moment in the limelight was over and he hadn't fluffed his lines.

His parents had smiled throughout the wedding service, and his mother had cried. Now, only he and his next youngest brother remained unmarried, and Hamish, now teaching in Stirling, at least had a girlfriend. His mother had been concerned when he'd split with Emily, but he couldn't go on lying to her, giving her hope their relationship might develop into something more. She deserved better than him telling her he didn't believe in sex before marriage. Sam hoped his God would understand his frailties. It was his fellow humans he was more uncertain about, even though the church had recently voted to allow ministers to have same-sex partners. The vote in the northeast of Scotland had been close, and Sam didn't want to rock the boat, so he remained firmly in his self-imposed closet.

* * * *

Finally, with the food and speeches over, and the dancing due to begin, Sam prepared to slip away after Gus and Mel had performed the first dance. He stood at the edge of the room, near the French windows, ready to make his getaway when he sensed someone behind him.

"They're good together, don't you think?"

Sam recognized the voice of Darach McNaughton, the man he considered his nemesis. The man who could take down his carefully organized world if he chose. Sam turned.

"Yes, they do. Gus is a lucky man, and they obviously adore each other. Where's *your* other half?"

"Over there talking to Davy and Jason."

Sam glanced to his left, where Brice Drummond sat in his wheelchair, deep in conversation with the other two men. "So any plans to marry, Darach? I see you're wearing a ring."

"We're talking about it. I asked him and he said yes. We're thinking of having the ceremony at the Lodge, and Tosh has agreed to be my best man. I wasn't sure whether to ask him, but he said he'd be upset if I asked anyone else."

"That sounds like Brodie." He used the name deliberately, knowing he was the only person who hadn't chosen to use his nickname. Somehow it made Sam feel closer to him. "He's an understanding man." Sam spoke thoughtfully, not wanting to give anything away.

"I've noticed you've been spending a lot of time with him. Tosh says you've been his rock since Harry's death, and he's joined your congregation. His mother must be pleased he's attending a church, even if it's not a Catholic one. Strange, I never had Tosh down as a God-botherer, but I suppose grief gets people in different ways."

"Everyone who finds their way to God has their own reasons," Sam replied.

Darach stared at him, and heat spread up Sam's neck and into his cheeks, fortunately covered by his beard.

"I suppose they do, but I have to admit I was surprised to find out you'd become a minister and returned home. Tosh told me you'd split with your girlfriend recently. I'm sorry to hear that."

Sam couldn't miss the tone of Darach's voice — the doubt he expressed spoken so clearly. "These things happen. The life of a minister's wife isn't for everyone."

"No, I suppose not. Just like being straight isn't for everyone."

Sam tensed. He didn't want to talk about their past, especially here at his brother's wedding. He glanced to his left to see Brodie heading his way.

"You don't need to worry. He's totally in the dark regarding what you and me used to get up to in the PE cupboard. I've no idea what's going on with you, Sam, but if you hurt him, I'll tear you limb from limb, policeman or not. He's vulnerable and too caring."

"We're friends, Darach, and that's all we'll ever be."

"Even if you want more?"

Sam swallowed hard. "Even if I want more. The reality of my situation is perfectly clear to me. I made a choice and became a minister. You might think it's mad, but I *was* called to this role. You have your vocation, and I have mine."

Tosh appeared in front of them. "I might have guessed I'd

find you two skulking in the shadows. Brice said I should ask you to dance, Dar, as he wants to watch you shaking your arse, so I'm here to drag you onto the dance floor." He turned toward Sam. "And what about you? Fancy a turn?"

"No, you go with Darach. I have two left feet, and I don't think it would be appropriate for me to shake my arse, do you? I'm sure your mother would have something to say if a minister took to the dance floor and strutted his stuff."

"Shame," Darach said. "You always had a great arse."

Sam managed a slight smile but avoided looking at Brodie's reaction to Darach's comment.

Darach grabbed his friend's hand. "Come on then, Tosh. Let's show this lot how *gay* men dance." Darach pulled him onto the dance floor. As they moved around each other, Darach kept glancing his way. Sam's heart sank. He dug his hands deep into his pockets and sighed.

"You look as if you need a stiff drink, bro." Sam looked up at the sound of at his oldest brother's voice. Alec held his two-year-old daughter in his arms. "Here, you hold Jenny and I'll get us a couple of pints. Sandie's determined to get me up dancing. Thankfully, this little one needed the loo, so I volunteered to take her."

His niece reached out her arms and Sam lifted her from his brother. Alec had three children, two boys and Jenny, the youngest, and if Sam had to admit it, being the only girl, his favorite.

Sam found a seat in a corner away from the dancing. He bounced Jenny on his knee, making her giggle. Opening her palm, he drew circles with his fingers and sang, "Round and round the garden like a teddy bear—one step, two step—and tickle you under there." He tickled under her arm, and she laughed and squirmed before demanding more. At least, not expecting to ever have children of his own, he could be the doting uncle. Alec appeared and put a pint in front of him.

"You spoil her," he said.

"Well, she's special. The first female Carmichael born

9

in three generations." Sandie appeared out of the crowd. "Here, I'll take her." She lifted Jenny out of his arms. "I'm going to take the three of them home now. Linda volunteered to babysit." She turned to her husband. "So I'll be back to get *you* on the dance floor later. Don't drink too much. You've work in the morning, and I don't want you chopping off anything vital." She kissed Alec and, carrying Jenny, left them together.

"I saw you talking to Darach and Tosh earlier. What is it with you and Sergeant McNaughton? You're always tense when he's around. I remember how you reacted when I told you he'd returned home. You turned white as a sheet."

Sam struggled to control the rising panic in his chest and swallowed several large mouthfuls of beer in an effort to calm himself. "It's nothing. We fell out at school and, with him coming back like the prodigal son, and what happened to Brodie's husband, something about him rubs me up the wrong way."

Alec didn't look convinced. "That's another thing. What's with you calling Tosh, Brodie? No one else does. Even his parents call him Tosh. And you've spent a lot of time with him since Harry died."

His patience snapped. "You mean since that gang murdered him."

"I realize the circumstances weren't normal, but you two weren't especially friendly before, and he didn't even attend church."

Sam willed himself not to blush. "He does now and it's my job to help the bereaved. Brodie is a good man. No one should have to go through what happened to him, getting caught up in someone else's problems like he did." Out of the corner of his eye, he spotted Darach gazing at him. Alec followed his view.

"This 'thing' that happened between you in school?" Sam glanced at the table.

"Leave it, Alec. There's nothing to talk about. I made a mistake, that's all. The way he dumped Brodie when he trooped off to university spoke volumes. He needed to have a little more humility. Perhaps now that he's with Brice, he won't be such an arrogant bastard. I've no idea why Brodie has remained friends with him after everything that's happened. He's even agreed to be Darach's best man."

His brother glanced over to where Darach was shaking his arse while Tosh laughed. Bloody Darach McNaughton. How did *he* make Tosh laugh so much? Sam cursed himself for slipping back to *that* nickname. It wasn't fair, the easy way they had with each other, or how Darach touched him. He growled under his breath.

Alec thumped the table then grabbed Sam's arm. Sam tried to jerk it away. "Shit! That's it. How could I have been so blind? You and Darach McNaughton. Did he try it on with you in school? Is that it?"

Sam gripped the table, unable to face his brother. "Don't be so stupid."

"Look at me, Sam."

He ignored his brother's demand and continued to stare at the floor, willing Alec to shut up, desperate for his sister-in-law to return and take his brother away.

"You can't, can you? What are you hiding? What am I missing here?" He hesitated. "If he didn't try it on and you sent him packing then… Fuck me. You and him. You had something going on in school, didn't you? He knows you bat for both sides. Has he warned you to stay away from Tosh? Does he think you have an ulterior motive for befriending him?"

Alec sounded so pleased with himself, just like Hercule Poirot when he'd told everyone who had committed the crime then sat back and basked in the glory of his own deductions. Sam wanted the ground to open up and swallow him. His hand shaking, he put the glass on the table, afraid it might crack within his tight grip, and struggled to breathe as his brain tried to find an answer for his brother — one he might believe. No words came out of his mouth, but he found the strength to look up at last.

Alec's smile died immediately.

"It's all right, Sam. You've nothing to fear from me, but I'm right, aren't I? I can see it in your face. How long have you known you're bisexual? And why the hell didn't you tell me?"

Instinct took over. Sam rose and glanced around, searching for the nearest exit. Needing air, he rushed for the door, ripping his dog collar from his neck and opening his shirt. Once outside, he leaned over, placing a hand on each knee, trying to get his breath until he felt a hand on his back and he slumped down on a bench.

Chapter Two

Alec sat next to him. "For fuck's sake, Sam. Why didn't you tell me? You didn't have to keep it to yourself. I'd have listened. I don't care if you're straight, gay or bisexual, or anything else. You're my brother, and I love you. We stick together, us Carmichael boys, whatever life throws at us. You know, all for one and one for all. Always has been and always will be."

Sam wiped away his tears and stared down at the grass under his feet. Across the lawn, from inside the building, lights shone and the music played as if nothing had changed, when his whole life had been blown apart. He could deny it. He could try to persuade his brother he was wrong, but, without a doubt, his words of protest wouldn't be believed. The truth was, he wanted to talk to someone, and he trusted his eldest brother the most. Alec had taken care of them all. No one dared to have a go at one of the brothers with Alec around. He'd always been strong, working with their father from his early teens. His arms were huge and muscular. Sam had witnessed him wielding a cleaver taking apart an animal carcass many times.

"What was I supposed to say?" he asked.

"Hi, my name is Sam Carmichael and I fancy men," Alec suggested.

Sam managed a chuckle and peeked up for the first time to see the concerned expression on his brother's face. "Hi, my name is Sam Carmichael, and I'm gay."

"Just gay? What about Emily and the others?"

"I suppose there is the remote possibility I may be bisexual. I mean, I like women, but I've never found one

13

I've wanted to sleep with. I finished with Emily because I couldn't deceive her any longer. I've been such a hypocrite."

"Bloody hell, Sam. I'm so sorry you didn't feel you could talk to me. It never even crossed my mind you might be."

"That was my plan. I had to do something so people wouldn't speculate. It's easier to use the no sex before marriage excuse when you're a minister."

"But not so easy to come out. You didn't exactly choose the best job."

He stiffened, waiting for the inevitable comment about the church, but none came. "I didn't choose the church, Alec. It chose me. When I hightailed it to university to get away from here, I could finally do what I wanted, which turned out to be—so many men, so little time." He didn't want to give Alec any more details—not yet. "But then I got involved with a local LGBT youth center for teenagers who had been chucked out by their parents and ended up on the street. One of the people who worked there was a minister I talked to at a church near university. Turned out he was the chaplain. I spent a lot of time talking to him and the kids, and I suppose you could say I saw the light. I swapped courses and studied theology, attended church." All right, maybe that wasn't the whole truth, but it would do for now. "It wasn't always easy, and it still isn't, but I don't regret my decision. I've found my vocation in helping others."

"And Darach McNaughton?"

"You were right. Me and him messed about back in school. A bit of mutual masturbation and a few blow jobs. I was a year older than him, but we were both under age. Then he got together with Brodie, and I hurried off to Glasgow. But he's the one person around here who knows my secret. I always worried he'd tell Brodie, but it appears he never did."

"And Tosh? You have feelings for him, don't you?"

Sam nodded. "I tried not to. I really tried, Alec. You have to believe me."

"I do, Sam. You wouldn't do anything lightly, or without care."

"The man only lost his husband a year ago, and here I am mooning after him like a lovesick teenager. I can't get him out of my head. I make excuses to see him, and I'm sure Darach has guessed. What if he tells Brodie?"

"What if he does? Tosh can decide for himself. You've spent a lot of time together since Harry died."

"Yeah, when I was supposed to be helping *him*, not myself." He breathed in and let out a long breath as he slumped. "It's no good. I've left it too late. How could I come out now? And if I did, I have no idea if he has any feelings for me. I see his face when he talks about Harry. I'm his friend, and if Darach tells him I'm simply being kind to get into his pants, he'll never trust me again." He leaned on his knees with his head resting in his hands.

"But what are you going to do? It'll drive you mad to be so close to him and only be friends. Eventually, he'll move on and find someone else. Could you stand that, Sam?"

"I'm thinking of asking for a transfer, maybe to a city parish where I can go back to working with lost teenagers and do some good, rather than here, where the biggest worry is who is on the church cleaning rota. I haven't done anything to help those in need around here, the drug addicts, the homeless, et cetera. All I do in the schools is talk religion and pray."

"You're too hard on yourself, as usual. I've no idea what to suggest concerning Tosh, but I don't want you to go anywhere else, and you're too young to give up on a chance of happiness. I'd be lost without Sandie and the kids. And the family would be fine if you told them you're gay."

"Really? Are you that naïve? I'd be letting Mum and Dad down, not to mention Granny. Can you imagine how she'd react? The church is all I have, Sam. It's important to me. I realize some people don't understand how I can believe in something I've never seen, but that's what faith is about. No, I'll go on as I have been for now. Please don't tell anyone else. Well, maybe Sandie, but no one else."

"I think you're wrong, but no, I won't tell anyone other than Sandie. She'll be fine and I don't like keeping secrets from her."

The door opened, sending a beam of light across the lawn in their direction. Sam glanced up. Brodie stood framed by the door then sashayed toward them rather unsteadily. "There you are. I thought you'd gone home to avoid our dance."

A winning smile followed Brodie's slurred words. Sam's heart swelled then melted. He wanted nothing more than to take Brodie in his arms, feel his head on his shoulder, and to sway slowly together to the music.

"I told you, two left feet, but let's get you back in." He crossed the space to the door and helped Brodie back to a seat inside.

"You've been so good to me, Sam, and listened to me going on about Harry. I don't know how I'd have coped without you." Brodie lay his head on Sam's shoulder.

"Should I take him home?" he asked Alec when he appeared beside him.

"I'll tell anyone who asks. Go on, take care of him, and make sure he's safe. Prop him up, you know. Maybe you should stay with him, just in case. Here, I'll help you get him to your car."

Sandie arrived as they put Brodie in the front seat. Sam waited while his brother talked, noting her glance in his direction, then he drove away with Brodie slumped beside him.

Getting Brodie up the narrow stairs proved tricky, but having removed his outer clothing, Sam laid him down on his side in case the amount of alcohol he'd drunk made him sick. He placed pillows behind him to stop him rolling over onto his back, and sat in the armchair in the corner, watching the room. Every so often, Brodie moaned and moved around, but eventually both succumbed to the need to sleep.

* * * *

When Tosh woke, his mouth tasted rank and his head thumped. He sat up and wiped his eyes, noting the pillows behind him, and that he wore only his boxers. He'd drunk way too much the night before. He picked up the photograph of Harry he kept by his bedside and stroked it as he did every morning. He needed a shower and tea, and not necessarily in that order.

It took him a while to work out that the buzzing noise wasn't in his head, but came from his phone. He picked it up from the bedside table and noted the plethora of texts from Darach asking if he was all right. He searched his contact list and rang his friend.

Darach gave him no chance to speak. "Where the hell have you been? I've been texting you all night. I was worried. Last I'd heard, you'd gone off with Sam Carmichael."

"Morning to you too. I'm fine. I had too much to drink, so Sam brought me home and took care of me."

"Took care of you how?"

"Got me undressed and put me to bed." The sound of pans crashing and a curse sounded from downstairs. "And from the noise I hear, Sam's downstairs attempting to make breakfast."

"You're okay, though. You can remember what happened when you arrived home?"

"Vaguely, I dozed off as soon as I laid down. Bloody wedding. Too many memories."

"You should have come to us. We'd have taken care of you. He's always hanging around like a bad smell."

"What *is* your problem with Sam? I've never understood. I know you're a dyed-in-the-wool atheist, but you're sounding a tad obsessed, Dar. Anyone would think you were jealous or something." Tosh couldn't help but feel puzzled. The tension between his best friend and Sam was palpable every time they met.

"I'm concerned about his motives, and you've been

17

attending his church."

"I go because I find it soothing, not because I've found religion or anything. It gives me space to contemplate the universe, and I like listening to Sam. His voice calms me. I don't listen to everything he says, but he helps me to put everything into perspective, and stops me blaming others for what happened to Harry. You should feel grateful to him, not suspicious. Anyway, I'm all right, and now I need to clean my teeth and drink a lot of tea. I'll see you soon. I'm back at work tomorrow, so I'll be passing your way. I could drop in for a quick drink, then."

"Take care of yourself. I worry about you."

"I know you do, Dar. And I love you too. Now, go and take care of your boyfriend, and feed your poor starving cat who's been meowing pitifully throughout this call."

Tosh pressed the red button and stared at the wall. *Weird. Why do I get the feeling I'm missing something? Maybe I'll ask Sam what the problem is, because something's going on.*

After visiting the bathroom, Tosh threw on his dressing gown, then made his way down the narrow stairs to the kitchen.

Sam stared at him when he appeared. "I thought you'd be dressed," he said.

Tosh glanced down at his bare legs and feet and pulled the cotton dressing gown across his chest, feeling suddenly uneasy at the way Sam stared at him before turning back to the stove.

Tosh sat at the table. "I needed tea more, and is that scrambled egg on toast?"

"I thought you could do with some food in your stomach. How's your head?"

"Thumping a bit. I'll take a couple of painkillers after I've eaten. Thank you for taking care of me last night. You didn't have to stay."

"I was worried. I've known people drown in their own vomit by lying on their backs."

Tosh stretched over and put a hand on Sam's arm, but

pulled it back when Sam tensed under his touch. "Well, thank you anyway. You didn't have to. You've been good to me since Harry died, and I want you to know I appreciate it."

"It comes with the job description." Sam placed the egg on toast and put the plate in front of Sam. "Now, sit there and eat something. I'll make us tea then leave you to your day. I'm sure you have plans that don't need me hanging around."

Today of all days, Tosh didn't want to be by himself. Today was the day he'd first met Harry three years before, when he'd delivered the post to the new owner of the antiques shop. It hadn't exactly been love at first sight for either of them, and no one had been more surprised than him when he'd said yes to Harry's dinner invitation. He and Harry hadn't exactly been opposites. In fact, they'd found they had more in common than others would imagine seeing them together, and Tosh had found himself becoming more eager to see him every day. Harry had flirted so obviously, but above all else, he'd made Tosh laugh. Indeed, he'd laughed him into bed and the sparks had flown. His cock stirred at the mere memory of that first night and the others that had followed. No, he didn't want to be by himself today. He'd done enough wallowing in self-pity.

He cleared his throat. "Do you fancy going somewhere later today after church? It's been ages since I've been out of town. We could have a run out to Lossiemouth beach. The sun is shining and there's enough breeze, judging by the way next door's washing is blowing about. It's just I have this stunt kite I've hardly used. Why don't you lose the minister's guise and wear civvies? Go on, indulge me."

Sam didn't answer straight away. Tosh guessed the man didn't get much opportunity to go out and simply have fun either.

"I'll need to go home first and change clothes," Sam said. "If you're sure you want my company."

"Of course I'm sure. Come on, Sam, live a little. I'm hardly inviting you to a gay club. When did you last fly a kite or have any real fun?" Tosh searched Sam's face, not sure of his expression other than he appeared to be fighting with himself. He crumpled slightly before straightening to his impressive full height, stroking his beard.

"Okay, why not? And the answer is—I can't remember ever flying a kite."

Chapter Three

"Could you make sure the kite doesn't try to get into the air while I sort out the lines?" Tosh asked.

Sam laid down the hand straps and covered them with sand, then walked slowly over the beach toward where Tosh stood unraveling the two guide lines.

"I never realized how much work flying a kite involved," Sam said as Tosh set up. "It's not merely paper and string, is it?"

"No, this is a proper stunt kite. Harry bought it for me just before…you know. This is the first time I've had it out." He remembered the morning of his birthday, a day he now preferred to forget as it coincided with Harry's death. They'd watched a documentary on TV a while before with people being pulled along the sand on wheels by huge power kites. Tosh had enthused about trying one out. Instead, Harry had presented him with the stunt kite as a starting point.

"Hold it while I attach the lines, will you?" Tosh made looped knots and secured each to the handles.

The strong breeze filled the kite and pushed against Sam.

Tosh edged back along the beach. "Keep hold of it tightly until I tell you to let go. You need to get it over your head and face into the breeze."

For a moment, Tosh stared as Sam held up the kite. He'd never seen Sam so casually dressed, without his standard dark trousers, dark shirt and clerical collar. The minister had always kept to his designated role when visiting Tosh, maintaining the distance between them. But now, with his dark blond hair and beard set off by beige cargo pants, white sleeveless T-shirt and trainer-style sandals, he appeared every inch a typical, laid-back hipster beach bum. It was quite a transformation and the outfit suited him, especially with the pale blue jumper slung around his shoulders and knotted across his chest. Tosh found himself assessing Sam in a way he'd never done before. Yes, he'd appreciated Sam's good looks—he wasn't blind. But with his height and lean frame, Sam was also eminently fanciable.

"I'm going to go farther back and take hold of the straps. I'll shout when I want you to let go, and once I've had it up a while, I'll show you how to do the stunt moves. At least there aren't many people around at this time of year before the school holidays."

As he trudged through the soft sand toward the sea, Tosh glanced down the long beach with the waves coming onto the sands. The only other visitors to the beach were dog walkers and a couple of people on horseback. He loved Lossiemouth. To get to the beach proper, visitors had to cross over a wooden bridge to the spit of land that separated the river from the firth. After the lunch they'd had at the café on the front, they'd needed to walk to a suitable spot, and soft sand had proved a challenge. He picked up the handles and wrapped the straps around his wrists.

"Okay," he shouted to Sam. "Hold it above your head and let go when I tell you."

"Like this," Sam shouted.

Tosh nodded and waited for the wind. "Now," he shouted. He stepped back and grinned as the straps pulled on his wrists and the kite soared up into the sky. Sam ran over and stood by his side as he practiced pulling each guide line a little at a time, making the kite turn one way then another.

"You're good," Sam said. "I can't believe how high they go."

"You can get these huge power kites with four ropes as well as brake and movement lines. I've always fancied kite buggying myself."

"What the hell is kite buggying?" Sam asked. "I've seen

them kite surfing around here and that looks scary enough."

"You attach a kite to a cart on wheels and they run along at great speed on a beach, but I'm not sure this one is long enough. It can be dangerous, though, if the wind is too strong. Right, let's see if I can make this thing swoop, or even make a figure of eight."

Tosh spent the next fifteen minutes making the kite move in each direction. "So if you keep going, you can do loops, but you have to count them and do it the same number the other way or the wires get tangled and can bring the kite down too quickly." Tosh glanced at Sam. "What's the matter?" he asked.

Sam shook his head. "Nothing."

Tosh glanced again, still trying to keep one eye on the looping kite. "Why are you smirking, then?"

"Me? I'm not smirking. I'm not sure I even know how to smirk, or, if as a man of the cloth, I'm allowed to smirk."

"Bloody hell, now see what you've done. You made me take my eye off it." The kite had plummeted to the sand some distance away. "I'll have to untangle the lines now, and it's your fault for distracting me. And you still haven't answered my question."

Sam walked backward. "It's nothing. But I could have sworn you only swung one way."

Open-mouthed and confused, Tosh watched him turn and run toward the fallen kite. Was Sam flirting with him? Had he just made a joke packed full of innuendo? As he gazed at Sam leaning over to scoop up the kite, Tosh realized he was staring at Sam's arse. Shit! He needed to get his act together.

Sam ran back toward him. His face flushed, he appeared somewhat sheepish. "I'll turn the kite while you unwind the lines, then maybe you could show me how to fly it?"

Tosh stared at Sam's arms then pushed away the sudden recognition of how strong they were, not overly muscular, but well-formed with a smattering of freckles which stretched up to his shoulders. "Yeah, your turn," he said, feigning concentration on his task.

It turned out Sam was a natural. Within ten minutes, he had the kite swooping across the sands, almost hitting the beach before soaring back up again. Tosh couldn't take his eyes off him, the wind ruffling his hair, an expression of total concentration on his face, like it was the first fun he'd had in ages, and maybe it was. He also scrutinized Sam's strong calf muscles as the man fixed his position on the sand, the surprisingly well-formed biceps exposed when he lifted his arms. Then there was the toned stomach also revealed as Sam struggled to keep control, with its trail of dark blond hair leading down. That he noticed this about Sam came as a surprise to Tosh. It was like seeing Sam for the first time, not as a minister or even as a friend but as a man. His cock, stirring in response, came as even more of a shock. For over a year, he'd felt nothing. He'd hardly bothered to masturbate, except on the odd occasion in an effort to wear himself out enough to sleep when alcohol hadn't worked. But now, he found the sight of Sam laughing and smiling made him want to do the same. Then pain hit his temple and he dropped like a stone.

"Brodie, oh hell. Tosh, speak to me. Are you all right? Have I killed you?" Sam wrapped his arms around him. "For God's sake, speak to me."

Tosh gazed up at Sam's concerned face and burst out laughing. "I'm fine. Just bruised." He rubbed the side of his head. "Kites have a sharp point when they hit you."

"I could have killed you."

Surprised by the genuine look of concern on Sam's face, Tosh placed his hand on Sam's arm. "Truly, I'm fine. Stop worrying." Sam then put his hand over Tosh's and, for a moment, they remained in that position.

"Shit, the kite." Tosh lunged to his left and grabbed the line before the kite blew away down the beach. "Come on. Let's pack away, cross back over the bridge and get an ice cream. There's a great place on the front, and we could sit on a bench and watch the world go by."

"You're sure you're okay?"

"Yes, I'll live, but you're paying for the ice cream and you can carry the kite."

* * * *

Tosh licked his cone and stared at the dog running to fetch the ball from the water. They were silent, but Tosh couldn't help being conscious of the physicality of the man sitting next to him.

"I can't remember the last time I sat on a bench, eating an ice cream and watching the world go by," Sam said.

Out of the corner of his eye, Tosh saw Sam extend his tongue to lick up the soft ice cream. He needed to change the subject. Dressed as he was, Sam had turned into a man, a very handsome man with a strong sense of humor. He'd escaped his box, and Tosh needed to put him back in the only way he knew how. "Do you enjoy being a minister?" he asked.

Sam shuffled and didn't reply immediately. "I'm not sure enjoy is always the word I'd use. Faith is peculiar. My family isn't religious. Mum and Dad attend every so often, more I suppose because they come to support me. My granny is a regular attendee and can be old-school about belief. I wanted to help people. At university, I made some bad choices, but then I met someone who listened. He didn't preach at me, or call me a terrible sinner bound for hell if I didn't repent my sins."

Tosh wondered what sins Sam had committed that required forgiveness.

"Through him I found peace and acceptance, and I found I wanted to give the same feeling to others. I will never be a hell and damnation preacher, like you see on those evangelistic TV shows. I believe most people are good and want to do good. Maybe it's naïve of me."

Tosh nodded, trying to take in Sam's words. "When you agreed to perform Harry's funeral, I was worried. Harry didn't parade his faith on his sleeve, but he believed passionately in forgiveness. He thought people were fragile in many ways and made mistakes, and therefore, that the writers of the Bible had made mistakes. To err is human and to forgive divine and all that. I don't think I ever heard him say a bad word about anyone. He often quoted Elizabeth I's view about opening a window into men's souls."

"It sounds to me as if we would have had a lot in common, Harry and me."

Tosh decided to provoke Sam, to check out his suspicions. "You've never said anything, you know, with regard to Harry and me being gay. The Bible says it's an abomination."

"No, it doesn't."

The ferociousness and speed of Sam's reply surprised Tosh. He'd obviously hit a nerve.

"Well, not in those exact words, and the Bible gives a lot of so-called rules. Jesus had nothing to say on the subject of homosexuality and…" He paused. Sam tensed next to him. Tosh glanced down to see Sam's hands balled into fists.

"Sorry," Sam continued. "I don't want to spoil our day and get into a theological argument about what the Bible says and what it doesn't. Do you mind?"

"My parents weren't too happy when I came out. As Catholics, they attended church and… Let's say our priest had different views to you. He told them I either needed to repent and change my ways, or be cast out. To begin with they followed his instructions, knowing I would go to Darach's house and be safe. Whenever I visited, they were uncomfortable around me, whereas Darach's mum and dad were great. Even after they spoke to my parents, and I returned home, I spent more time over at the farm than I did at home. Then Darach and I got together."

Sam squirmed again. And had he murmured something under his breath? Once again, Tosh guessed something had caused this animosity. He determined to get Darach to tell him the truth. After a long silence, Tosh became more and more conscious they hadn't made any eye contact since sitting on the bench.

"The chaplain I mentioned volunteered at a local shelter for homeless youth in Glasgow. Many of them were gay and had been thrown out. So many lives ruined."

Tosh sighed. "Sorry, I promised you a fun day out and this conversation has turned rather maudlin. I wanted you to know I've appreciated every time you listened to me since Harry died. I'm not sure I would have coped as well without you. You've been a good friend."

For the first time, Sam turned and gazed at him. "Are you trying to tell me you don't want me around as much anymore? Because I'll understand."

That's not what your panicked expression is saying. If I didn't know better... Tosh didn't want to go any further with that thought. "No, I like having you around, but I'm not over Harry yet. You understand, don't you?"

Sam's eyes widened, and Tosh knew he'd been right.

"I'm not going to say anything, Sam. If you want to talk, I'll be there. I've enjoyed today, but maybe it's time to go home. I'll see you on Sunday at church."

"You're still going to attend, then. I wasn't sure."

"Yes. I'm not sure why. I like the building, and your sermons make me think."

"I'm glad you find solace there, and that we can be friends. Some people find it hard to be friends with a minister. They imagine I'm going to blether on about God all the time, but we're human too. Sometimes very human."

Tosh spent the drive home in quiet contemplation while Sam stared straight ahead. He considered the man sitting next to him. He liked Sam. He liked him a lot. But he wasn't sure he was ready to move on. He guessed Sam had feelings for him from the expression on his face when he'd thought Tosh might be telling him he didn't want them to hang out together. But if Sam swung both ways, he was obviously deep in the closet, and Tosh didn't want to revisit a life of hiding his feelings. Sam would have to deal with his own demons until he was ready to talk.

"I'll see you on Sunday, then," Sam said after he emerged from the car.

Tosh wound the window down. "I meant what I said, Sam. If you need to talk, I'll listen."

A red flush spread up Sam's neck. Sam nodded at him, turned and walked to his door without looking back.

Chapter Four

When the doorbell rang on Saturday night, Tosh had just settled down with his feet up and a large bowl of homemade chicken curry. He sighed, wondering who it could be. When a key turned in the lock, he knew it could only be Darach. So much for a quiet evening in, indulging himself with a curry and *Star Wars*. He didn't get up. Their friendship had been somewhat frosty since Harry's death. It had taken time for him not to blame Darach, or his partner, Brice, but it was still difficult to separate them from the mindlessness of what had happened. Their presence was a constant reminder of his loss.

"I brought takeaway," Darach said. "But I see you have your own."

Tosh stood. "I can put this back in the saucepan and freeze it with the rest."

Darach smiled at him. This was yet another peace offering, and Tosh wasn't going to send his friend away. "Come on, then, hand it over. I'll get more plates. You'll have bought too much as always."

Darach handed over the bag and plonked himself down on the sofa. "Oh great, you're watching *Star Wars*. I can't get Brice interested at all."

Tosh brought the food and plates back in and they sorted out the different items between them. Darach made pancake rolls filled with crispy duck, cucumber and spring onion, and splashed with liberal amounts of hoisin sauce. His friend moaned out loud as he sank his teeth in.

"Oh, these are good. I daren't have duck at home. Brice stares at me as if I'm eating someone's pet. Sometimes it's hard living with a vegetarian."

"Where is Brice tonight?"

"He's working. I know. It's bloody typical. I get a Saturday night off duty and he has a big order to complete for Davy and Jason. He's creating these tiles for a kitchen they are fitting out, and having trouble getting the colors right. He told me my long face was distracting him and that I should go and annoy someone else with it, so I thought of you."

"I'm flattered, I'm sure," Tosh said. "You're right about the duck, though. It is bloody good. Ready to watch?"

For a while, Tosh ate with Darach in companionable silence, the only noise coming from the film and the scrape of cutlery on plates.

"I need another drink," Tosh said. "I'm going to make tea. Do you want some?"

"I'll bring in the leftovers," Darach said, collecting the various plastic boxes and plates.

"How's your mum?" Tosh asked, waiting for the kettle to boil.

"She has good and bad days. There's not a lot we can do. She tries to keep busy, but she knows as well as we do, she's going to get worse. Dementia is such a terrible condition. Dad's trying to be strong, but he's afraid of losing her as well. You'll have to come up and see them. You know they'd love to have you for dinner."

"I will. Your parents have always been good to me."

"They love you, that's why."

Tosh wiped away a tear from the corner of his eye. Darach's parents had never questioned their relationship when they were teenagers. They'd taken him under their wing when his parents had been uncertain what to do. Fortunately, his parents had come round, and although they weren't going to be waving a rainbow flag, or marching in a Pride parade any time soon, they'd accepted the situation and had been supportive after Harry's death.

Darach wrapped his arms around Tosh's waist and lay his head on his shoulder. Tosh sighed, happy that there was no more awkwardness between them. He'd missed his friend. "I'm trying to make tea," he said, pouring the water into two large mugs.

"Are you okay?" Darach asked, his arms still around Tosh.

Tosh patted his arm. "It gets easier. My birthday was tough. Not the best day to have your husband die. It's hard to believe it's been over a year now."

He picked up the tea and extracted himself from Darach's arms. "Come on, we have the rest of the film to watch."

Before he could press the on button, Darach spoke. "Is there something going on between you and Sam Carmichael?"

Tosh clutched his mug, stopping it slipping through his hand. "What? No! Why would you even think that?"

"I've noticed he's been hanging around here a lot, and you breezed off, out for the day, last week. You've also started going to church. You haven't got God, have you?"

Tosh guessed someone must have seen him and Sam out at the beach. Everyone knew everyone's business around here. He wasn't surprised.

"No, I haven't got God, as you so succinctly put it. I simply find it peaceful." He paused. "And Harry's never been there. I can't picture him in the church, so he stays in my head, like he does here, because he wasn't ever here either. Being anywhere he was is still painful. I can see him if I peer through the shop window on my round. I imagine him there behind the antiques bustling away, and I want to go in and give him a quick kiss before I'm on my way. I should be better by now. I tell people I am, and some days it's true. Sam's been good to me. He listens, and he's never told me to man up and move on. So you can take your warped imaginings and shove them where the sun doesn't shine." He gripped a cushion, wanting to throw it as anger surged through him, quickly followed by guilt because Darach might have a point.

"I care about you, Tosh. You're still my best friend."

"Oh yeah, I'm the best friend you ran out on for twelve

years. That's how much I mattered to you. And now you're all loved up with the man who killed my Harry."

"That's not fair, Tosh, and beneath you to even suggest it. It wasn't Brice's fault. He didn't kill Harry."

Tosh turned to stare at Darach. He spoke through gritted teeth. His fingernails buried deep into the flesh of his palms. "No, it's your fault. If you hadn't asked Harry to go over there, he would be alive now. It's your fault he's dead, Darach. Yours." Tears streamed down his face and he sobbed, unable to stop himself from shaking, even when he wrapped his arms around himself. This was the first time since last year he'd let his feelings run away. Darach's eyes widened with panic, his expression full of pain.

"I'm sorry, Tosh. If I could change what happened, I would. You know I would. I get how you blame me, and you're right. It was my fault. I didn't want to lose Brice."

"You see. This is my problem. I see you two together all happy and smiley, and I can't stand it. Sam didn't know Harry. He and I don't have a past like you and me. He's completely separate from everything that happened between us, and from Harry. Maybe he does see me as more than a lost sheep to be gathered into his fold, but he's never thrown God at me, or himself for that matter." Tosh wiped his face on his sleeve.

"You know he's gay, or bisexual," Darach said. "At school, he and I—"

Tosh didn't want to hear his suspicions confirmed, and he certainly didn't want to hear how Darach knew. He put his hands up.

"No, Dar. I don't want to know. You know he helped me after Harry. He listens and we see each other on Sundays and at weddings and funerals. Last week was a one-off outing. We both needed some time away from here. He carries none of my past baggage, and he doesn't share his. Whatever it is you know, keep it to yourself, and stop judging either of us. I don't care if you and he exchanged hand jobs, or if he's a screaming queen who wears lace undies under his robes. Despite his beliefs, he accepts me for who I am and doesn't judge. He once told me he didn't think it was his place to judge others for their frailties. He leaves such issues to God. You might want to think about that yourself before you accuse him of trying to get into my pants. I think you should go now."

"I'm trying to help, Tosh. I don't want to see you hurt. He's so far in the closet, I can't imagine him having the courage to come out. Maybe he does like women as well, but something in the way he stares at you when he thinks no one is looking, makes me concerned his intentions aren't as pure as you think they are."

Tosh frowned at him. "Go, Darach. Go back to your man. Love him while you still have him, because you never know what's around the corner."

"Are you forgetting? I nearly lost him too."

"But you didn't. You get to hold him every night in your arms when all I have when I go to bed is a photograph and my memories. I'm not going to jump into bed with Sam because he's there and Harry isn't, okay?"

"All right. I hear you. I know you're hurting. I meant it when I mentioned seeing my Mum and Dad. Don't cut them off because you're angry with me." Darach rose and headed to the door. "Take care of yourself. You know where I am if you want me."

Tosh waited until he heard the key in the lock from the other side and the noise of an engine starting, then he pressed the on button on his DVD player and sat watching the rest of the film.

Later, he sat on the edge of his bed and stared into space. He had to face Sam in the morning, and he wasn't sure what he would say. Was he attracted to Sam? In ordinary circumstances he could be. Sam was tall, slightly muscular and maybe a little too lean. With all the takeout he'd eaten recently, despite the amount of walking and cycling he did, Tosh knew he'd put on weight around his middle, not that he'd ever been thin. Harry had appreciated his love handles, and said his stomach made a lovely cushion. And there was Sam's beard, he definitely wasn't sure about that. It made him appear older. Maybe Sam thought it gave him more gravitas as a minister. Idly, he tried to imagine what it would be like to kiss Sam. Tosh had never kissed a man with a beard. Harry wouldn't even allow a fashionable degree of stubble to remain on his face. Would it be soft or wiry? Sam definitely kept himself in good shape if the view Tosh had received when the man had held on to the kite was to be believed. The sight of Sam's shirt riding up, exposing his abdomen, had certainly made Tosh's cock sit up and take interest.

He smiled to himself, remembering the moment he'd first realized he had feelings for Harry. Harry had fumbled with his glasses and dropped them when Tosh had appeared with his post dressed in his springtime shorts. They'd both reached to pick them up and stared at each other for a long time before standing. Tosh had asked Harry out to Moray Lodge for dinner. The first time they'd had sex had come later. Harry had proved to be a much different man in bed from the one he presented in his antiques shop. Gone was the seemingly priggish character with his glasses perched on the end of his nose, glaring at everyone, and, out of nowhere, appeared a man who took control in bed. Tosh had been bent practically double and left breathless, and what Harry could do with his tongue… Never had his arse received so much attention.

Tosh shifted on the bed, remembering the feel of just the tip pressing into him. He had to admit he'd loved finding out the naughty and wild side of the buttoned-up man the rest of the world had got to see. Blowing Harry while he'd stood behind the counter serving Mrs. Henderson, his mother's friend from church, had been an experience he'd treasure forever, and it was a shame no one would ever get to see one of Harry's favorite collections. Who knew you could get so many antique dildos and butt plugs? Tosh had especially loved the smoothness of the glass examples, and how cool they felt in his hands and up his arse. He wondered how Sam would react to the group of objects now stored at the bottom of the ottoman. Perhaps he should get them out and display them on his bedroom windowsill among his own *Star Wars* figures.

All this doesn't answer the problem of Sam, though, does it?

He needed sleep now. If he arrived late at church and got out early, he wouldn't have to speak to Sam. Sometimes he questioned why he was going at all. Part of him wanted to believe, but perhaps accepting the existence of an all-powerful being gave him someone else to blame for Harry's meaningless death. If he was right, and Sam harbored feelings for him, then he hoped he'd succeeded in letting Sam down gently. It was too soon. It might always be too soon.

Chapter Five

Sam put Jenny down on the floor and smiled as she toddled back to her father. She'd been slower to walk than her brothers, and for a while they'd worried over her development, but Ellis McKenzie had simply said she preferred getting around on her bottom and watching the world go by. Judging by her vocabulary, she listened a lot. You always had to be careful around her or you'd find her repeating choice phrases. When she reached his brother, she turned and waved at him, her blue eyes full of mischief. They were all in danger of spoiling the one girl in the family, which might turn out not be a good thing, considering her flaming red hair and the odd temper tantrum when she didn't get her way.

"Do you want a drink?" Alec asked.

"I'm fine with tea for now," Sam replied. "I'm not sure I could fit in anything else. Sandie does a great roast, and her crackling is to die for."

"McNaughton's pork, cut and prepared by yours truly — you can't beat it."

"The shop is doing okay, then?" Many local shops had struggled after the arrival of the big supermarkets in the area with their cheaper food.

"You can't beat quality. Rob Blair and I have been discussing setting up an online site to sell McNaughton Farm meat all over the country. I can butcher it and we split the profits. We have deals with most of the local hotels. Sandie has set up the website and pulled in a few other clients as well, working from home part-time. We've talked about setting up a cooperative with some of the other farmers and adding cheese and butter to our lists locally. But enough about us. What's the latest on you and our local postman? Anything new going on there after your trip to Lossie beach last week? You haven't said how it went."

"Nothing much to tell. We had a great day out. I nearly killed Brodie when I lost control of the kite and it hit him, knocking him down on the sand, and he told me, in no uncertain terms, that he wasn't over Harry."

"Shit!" He glanced down at his daughter snuggled next to him on the sofa. "Bugger. I hope she didn't hear that one."

"Or that one," Sam said, grinning.

"Did you tell Tosh you were gay?"

"No, not exactly, but he's not stupid. I might have made my feelings more obvious than I meant to. I caught him checking me out a few times. I thought... But what's the point? He's hardly going to want a secret affair with the local minister who is totally in the closet and paranoid about anyone finding out. There are simply too many complications. I must be mad imagining there could be something between us."

"Are you going to tell Stu, Gus or Hamish? I'm happy to keep your secret. But there's Mum and Dad as well. I'm sure they'd be all right. I bet they'd be less surprised than when you announced you'd decided to study theology. We've never been a church-going family, much to Granny's dismay. She's always been so proud of you, but then you were always her favorite."

"I don't think Granny would be pleased to find out her precious wee one is a poofter, do you?"

Jenny stirred on the sofa and opened her eyes. "Poofter," she said quietly.

"Oh, hell. Now I'm going to have to explain this one to everyone. Come on, young lady. Let's take you outside to play with your mum and brothers, shall we?"

Sam sat back in the armchair. Brodie had hardly even glanced at him during the church service. He'd arrived late and sat at the back. Sam had to face facts. Even if Brodie did like him, there were other complications and other hurdles to be overcome. Some people might be willing to accept his sexuality but… No, he pushed the thoughts aside. It was time to see Jock again. He'd go to Glasgow and visit him at the LGBT center. Jock always knew the right thing to say, and it would be good to catch up with the others and find out how they were doing.

"Penny for them," Alec said, bringing him out of his daydream.

"Oh, nothing. I was thinking I'd go and pay a visit to my old mentor back in Glasgow, the one I mentioned to you. It's been a while since I've spoken to him. He preached love and inclusiveness at a time when I needed to hear it."

"Is he gay?"

Sam bristled, annoyed at his brother's automatic assumption. "Jock? No. He's married with a daughter. I wish there were more like him in the world. His example is one of the reasons I'm hoping to set up a youth club to give the kids somewhere to go to and stop them from hanging around on the streets." Sam clocked his brother's worried frown. "I'm all right, you know. Some days are harder than others. I'm not unhappy, just not always happy. Let's go outside while the sun is shining and play with the boys, shall we?"

Alec nodded. "I can't help worrying. It's part of being the eldest. Mum and Dad always told me I had to take care of you."

"And you do, Alec. I'm glad we can talk. I hated hiding from you."

He stood and followed Alec out to the garden. The boys were on the swings set up near the back of the large lawn. Jenny sat in the sandpit digging with a bucket and spade while Sandie read from her Kindle. He strolled over and sat with Jenny in the pit, not caring if he got covered in sand. "Come on, then," he said, picking up the bucket. "Let's make a huge castle."

* * * *

A week later, overwhelming feelings of guilt assailed Tosh as he gazed at Sam shaking hands with the congregation members on their way out of the church. He hadn't meant to behave in such a cowardly fashion, but he found he couldn't face making small talk about the sermon and its theme of being a good neighbor. As Sam had stood in the pulpit, tall and commanding over his flock, Tosh had allowed himself a few glimpses, hoping Sam wouldn't meet his eye. Totally confused about his own feelings as well as Sam's, he'd baulked at even shaking his hand and ran for his car as soon as the service was over. He wanted to believe. He wanted to imagine Harry somewhere, assessing the value of God's many antiques, or discussing the state of the world with other like-minded people, as well as watching over him. But then again, he didn't want Harry hearing his thoughts. He didn't think Harry would want him to be lonely, but how soon was too soon to have those sort of thoughts about another person? Maybe if he asked, he'd get an answer.

Tosh put the car into gear and headed down the coastal road to the small parking spot where the seals hauled themselves out onto the rocks. Here he'd scattered Harry's ashes into the sea. Often they'd brought sandwiches and sat watching, hoping to catch a glimpse of dolphins, or even a whale, off the coast, as well as observing the many seals. Being there made him feel closer to Harry, even if the memories sometimes brought tears to his eyes.

Turning right into the small unofficial carpark, Tosh noted the other car already parked in the space, but deliberately didn't check on the occupants. Instead, he stared through the windscreen at the sea. The tide was on its way out, from what he could tell, gradually revealing the rocks the seals chose to sit on. The warmth of the day allowed walkers to remove their coats, despite the light breeze which rustled the long grass to his side. Gulls swooped overhead, joined by the occasional shag or cormorant. A few oystercatchers dodged to and fro as the waves came in. He opened the door and walked the few steps to the picnic table, sat on the bench, closed his eyes and turned his face to the sun. Didn't they say getting vitamins from sunshine was good for you?

The car next to his drove off but another soon took its place.

"Tosh, are you all right?"

He opened his eyes and turned to see the driver of the new car still winding down his window. Part of him slumped when he saw the occupant — Brice Drummond. He couldn't ignore *him*.

"I'm fine," he replied. "I thought I'd come and stare at the seals. What brings you here?"

"Darach is working, so I thought I'd bring my camera and sketch pad. If I position the car at the right angle, I don't have to get out. It's not the best place for managing a chair."

Tosh glanced down at the grass-covered gravel with its pot holes. "No, I don't suppose it is. Are you painting anything in particular?"

"I'm hoping to get photos of the seals, and the beach with different types of birds. The sea's calm today, so no great waves to capture. It's a good place to come and sit. I've brought sandwiches if you'd like something to eat. Only cheese and coleslaw, I'm afraid."

"That's right, you're a vegetarian." He chuckled. "I doubt you'll be able to persuade Darach to give up his meat."

Brice grinned. "I wouldn't want him to give up meat entirely."

Unable to stop himself, Tosh laughed. "I suppose I left myself open for that one. As I remember, he always did have a fondness for sausages."

"I've even sneaked in an occasional slice of vegetarian bacon, but don't tell him I said so."

Tosh chuckled at the thought. "I promise, I won't. And a sandwich would be great. I came here on the spur of the moment after church, so I didn't bring anything."

"I've got a couple of bottles of water as well."

Tosh stood and collected the sandwich and bottle. One taste told him the origin of the bread. "Maggie's walnut loaf goes well with this cheese," he said after chewing slowly.

Silence filled the gap between them as they ate staring out to sea, both well aware of the Darach-shaped elephant in the car park. Brice spoke first.

"He misses you. He's worried you're so angry with him that you won't see him again. I didn't know if you wanted to talk about what happened."

It had been a year. He'd avoided being on his own with Brice and declined every invitation from Darach to share a meal with them. He didn't want to sit down to dinner in the house where Harry had died, and he didn't want to entertain in the house he still rented from Darach. He'd insisted on paying him enough to cover the mortgage.

"I'm not truly angry with him," Tosh said. "I was angry with everyone to begin with, and he had you. Harry's was such a stupid death, but I suppose all deaths are full of if onlys. I can't even begin to imagine what you had to cope with."

"I try not to dwell on the past, but I have a great therapist, and I talk to her. It can be good to talk to people. I expect the reverend is a good listener."

Tosh jerked his head up. "He told you about me and Sam, then. He seems to think Sam is going to take advantage of me. Did he also tell you about *him* and Sam?"

"We've told each other everything."

"Of course you have. I had my suspicions at the time. I saw them sneaking out of the PE cupboard once or twice. But *my* relationship with Sam is none of his business, or yours. Whatever his feelings are for me, I've told him I'm not interested."

Brice stared at him. Tosh noted that he styled his hair differently now. Having let it grow out at the sides, it was cut shorter on top. It made him appear younger. Today he wore no makeup and his bright blue V-necked T-shirt revealed some of his many tattoos.

"Is that the truth, though? I have no right to question what you're saying, but being alone is hard, and he appears to be a genuine bloke, despite his church connections. I've never had much time for organized religion. Darach said you'd attended church a few times recently."

Tosh wanted to tell Brice to shut up, but tiredness overwhelmed his anger. He *was* lonely, and he missed waking up next to someone, eating with someone, having someone to come home to after his round. People didn't know what to say to him. Even his parents struggled to help. Sam was the one person he'd been comfortable with, and now he faced losing him as well, because he didn't want to lead Sam on, or have a relationship with someone in the closet.

"Sam has been great, but it's complicated. Even if I were ready to move on from Harry, he's not out. Maybe the church allows ministers to have same-sex partners now, but I can imagine the faces of some in the congregation if Sam announced he was gay, and I'm not prepared to scuttle around in secret and have it blow up in our faces. No, we both have too much baggage, so it's better to stop before we give in to temptation."

"So you are tempted, then?"

Tosh buried his head in his hands.

"I'm sorry. Ignore me. I should learn to keep my mouth shut."

"Of course, I'm tempted. Who wouldn't be? He's tall, blond and handsome, even with the beard. He's kind and caring and so tolerant of the old ladies in his fan club. He's built up the congregation and brought younger people into the church, and he's hoping to get the school involved in setting up a youth club. You're right, being alone is hard, but it's useless. There's no future in it, and I can't face being hurt again."

He stood. "Thanks for the sandwich. I hope you get some good photographs. I love your work. Harry always said you had talent. It must be wonderful to be able to produce beautiful creations. I'll leave you to it."

"Don't give up on him too quickly," Brice said. "People manage to overcome all sorts of obstacles to find love." Brice gestured, indicating his chair. "I had a lot of baggage when Darach and I got together, which became public knowledge. It wasn't easy for him to deal with everyone knowing what I'd done, and how I'd lived. Every day he sees my past written all over me. Every day he has to deal with the practicalities of living with me and walk the tightrope of understanding when to help and when to leave me be. And every day he tells me he loves me. Perhaps you and Sam... Well, miracles do happen. "

"I hear what you're saying, but I'm not going to hold my breath. Tell Darach if he wants to come round, I won't bite his head off. We've known each other far too long to hold grudges forever."

He climbed into his car and negotiated his way out of the small space. If Sam wanted anything to change between them, *he'd* have to make the first move.

Chapter Six

Two months later

"But she's only going to see Aunty Lyn." Tosh paced his parents' living room. "The funeral is in forty-five minutes, and I don't want to have to sneak into the back."

"You know what she's like, son. Her and your aunty have been like this for years — the right outfit, shoes, makeup — always the same."

Tosh nodded. "You all right, Dad?"

"You know me, laddie. I'm a pebble on a beach. I let the tide go over and go back. Your mum says she's smoothed off my rough edges."

A door creaked as it opened across the hall.

"See, here I am. The hot weather's thrown me and I had to rethink my outfit."

Tosh closed the gap between them and kissed his mother's cheek. "You look lovely, Mum, as always."

She held him at arm's length. "Are you eating properly? You've lost weight in your face. Don't you think he's lost weight, Archie? You'll come over here at the weekend, and I'll do us a roast. Roast beef and all the trimmings."

"I'm fine, Mum, and we need to go."

"You're such a thoughtful boy, going to Mrs. Ramsay's funeral. I raised you well. And you're such a handsome sight in a suit and tie."

Tosh suppressed a chuckle. When he'd come out to his parents, his mother had said it was impossible for a good Catholic boy to be gay — that God wouldn't have allowed it. His father had simply shrugged and hugged him, but he had supported him when his mother had paraded 'nice' girls from 'good' families in front of him in the hope they might change his inclinations. She'd accused Darach of leading him astray. Now, she accepted his 'lifestyle choice' as she called it, and he had to agree she and Harry had got on well. Harry had been skilled at the type of flattery his mother required.

"You'll be seeing the Reverend Carmichael today. You haven't mentioned him for a while. I had hopes with you going to church, you might come back to the True Faith, but I suppose any faith is better than none at all. He's very popular. The old ladies love him when he goes to visit them at the home, and he's such a handsome man, even with a beard."

She fixed him with one of her questioning stares, and he gulped. Did she know? Could mothers tell? Did they have special powers? No, she hadn't guessed *he* might be gay, or so she'd said.

"I'm not sure faith is for me after all, Mum. And I'm going to the funeral to make sure there are a few people there. Mrs. Ramsay used to make a great mug of tea, and her ginger cake was to die for. At least her son got here. I know how much she missed him."

She placed a hand either side of his face. "You should get out there again and find someone, Brodie. You're still young, and Harry wouldn't have wanted you to fade away. I remember him telling me how much he liked a man with a bit of flesh on him."

Heat rushed up his neck and into his cheeks as he recalled *that* conversation at their first Christmas as a married couple between his mother, drunk on too many snowballs, and a tipsy Harry, whose wink had made her giggle like she was a teenage girl again.

"Mum! Really?"

"You know I'm right. If I can't persuade you to find a nice young lady, then I want you to be happy and find a nice man with whom you can have babies, and make me a granny."

"You do know two men can't make a baby, don't you?" Tosh replied, laughing at his father huffing in the corner.

"I've read about these celebrities in the magazines at the home. And any baby of yours would be so bonny. Now, look at the time. We're going to be late."

His father rose from his chair and followed them out. "Over the last thirty-five years, I've learned not to argue with your mother and she's right. You're young enough to start again and I think you'd make a great father."

On the drive to the church, after dropping his parents off and waving at his aunty as she hustled them into her well-appointed house, his thoughts dwelled on what his mother had said. He and Harry had discussed having kids, and he'd been all for it. When he pulled up outside the church, he climbed out of the car and hurried down the path, past Sam without speaking, seconds before the funeral party arrived, then waited to follow the mourners in.

Tosh pulled at his collar and wiped his brow. Around him stood a dozen or so people grateful for the cool of the church rather than the unusually warm weather outside. Mrs. Ramsay's coffin lay on its trolley at the front of the church while Sam Carmichael eulogized the old lady Tosh had delivered mail to since he'd started his job over thirteen years ago. She'd often given him a cup of tea on cold mornings, and he'd chatted to her. Adam, her son, stood at the front with his wife, having traveled from New Zealand for the occasion. Still, she'd had a good innings, making it to over ninety with all her faculties.

Every once in a while, he caught Sam glancing over at him. It had been two weeks since he'd stepped foot in the church, having recognized Sam was his reason for being there, not any sense of belief. He'd tried, but in the end, he'd decided the ability to have faith was beyond him, unlike Mrs. Ramsay, who'd been a regular churchgoer. At least it meant Sam knew the woman he was eulogizing.

Service over, Tosh joined the rest of the group moving

slowly behind the coffin. He didn't intend to go to the interment at the small cemetery overlooking the sea on the coastal road, or the gathering organized for afterward, so he shook hands quickly and walked out into the heat of the sun. Standing for a few moments, he undid his tie and placed it in his pocket.

"Our meetings have been limited to church lately," a voice behind him said quietly.

He turned to face Sam.

"Although it's been a few weeks since I've seen you on a Sunday. I would have been worried, except I see you every day on your round. So we've done a wedding and a funeral. A christening will give us the full set."

Tosh wasn't sure what to say. Having Sam so close to him caused butterflies to beat their wings in his chest and belly. Sam had stepped into his personal space as if he belonged there. Tosh was close enough to smell his aftershave mixed with a slight hint of perspiration. Wearing a black cleric's outfit with its tight white collar must have been difficult on such a warm day, but Sam appeared the epitome of cool, standing there with his hands clasped in front of him. In the end, Sam broke the silence.

"I've missed you. I've missed my visits and our chats. Can't we at least be friends? I'm not going to fling myself at you."

The whispered deep voice made Tosh's cock stir in his pants. Oh hell, why did this man affect him so? He answered before his brain had even reached first gear.

"Maybe the problem is I want you to." *Shit! Why did I say that?*

Sam whipped his head around, eyes wide with shock.

I've got to get out of here. Someone pulled him back as he moved forward.

"You can't say that and leave," Sam said

Tosh glanced over at the hearse. "I think you're the one who has to leave. They're waiting for you."

"This isn't over," Sam said. "I can't get you out of my

head."

"Come over to mine Friday night." Perhaps if he scratched the itch it would get it out of the way. His arse clenched at the thought of Sam with all his weight on top of him.

"I'm not sure that's a good idea."

"Be there," Tosh said, his voice almost a growl.

Sam raised a hand to acknowledge the waiting group. "All right, I'll be there at eight."

Tosh slumped against the wall as Sam hurried along the path and got into the car. *What the hell have I done?* Instinctively, he gazed up at the clear blue sky. Funny how he still did that, even if he didn't believe there was a heaven, or that Harry was up there sitting on a fluffy cloud watching over him. He had no doubt Harry would tell him to get on with life, and maybe it was time, even if feelings of guilt nibbled at his brain. At least the house he lived in had no residue of the man he'd loved so much. If sex was on the agenda, he'd rather do it without having a sense of Harry all around him, regardless of everything they'd said to each other.

* * * *

Fuck! Sam mouthed a silent sorry, glanced up then did as the note on the door instructed – locked up behind him and leaned back against it. What the hell was he doing? His head screamed for him to turn away, but the combination of love and lust had so far won the battle.

"Up here."

He stared up the stairs, both terrified and excited about what he might find when he got there, half of him wanting to bolt, the other half desperate to at least see and touch. Maybe he could… It had been so long. He couldn't believe how long. Yes, he'd been tempted, but he hadn't given in with so much at stake. But, before anything could happen between them, they needed to talk, or more importantly, *he* needed to talk. He put one foot on the bottom stair and a shaking hand on the rail. One by one, he took each step until he reached the top.

"In here," a familiar voice said from within the first room on the landing. The door was ajar, but he couldn't see inside. He swallowed hard and shuffled the few steps to the entrance, finally taking a step inside.

"Fuck!"

"That's the general idea. Like what you see?"

Sam stood rooted to the spot. Unable to move or speak, he nodded. Unconsciously, he wetted his lips, already semi-hard from the sight of Tosh lying completely naked on his front with his head peering over his shoulder staring at him, daring him.

"Well, are you going to simply stand there?" Tosh said. "This is what you wanted, isn't it? What we both wanted."

No, this was too fast. He needed to slow things down. "I can't. I didn't expect. Oh, God, Tosh." He stared at Tosh's legs with their strong calves from the years of walking and cycling, then up toward his fleshy arse. He could simply part those cheeks and sink himself into a warm body. But this wasn't *any* body—this was Tosh. This wasn't a simple fuck. It was the most complicated fuck he'd ever had.

Tosh's expression softened and he dragged his legs around to sit on the edge of the bed. Sam liked that he wasn't ripped with prominent muscles or a six pack. Tosh was ordinary, his body several shades lighter than his face, lower arms and legs, with a smattering of dark hair between the nipples down to where his cock lay heavy, surrounded by curls between his legs.

Tosh patted the bed. "That's the first time you've called me Tosh. Come here and sit next to me. I'm feeling rather underdressed now, and something of an idiot."

Sam closed the distance between them and sat next to Tosh. He gazed at the pattern of swirls on the carpet, unable to face the man. He searched for a reason as fear grabbed him by the throat. Even if he was careful, Tosh deserved honesty.

"This is wrong," he said. "I can't take advantage of you, not while you're grieving. I'm not sure you'll ever be over Harry."

"Isn't that my decision? Maybe I need this. Maybe I need to be full of something — someone — and not simply self-pity. Harry isn't coming back, and I need to move on. And perhaps you should try something other than self-loathing. Hating yourself because you're gay isn't healthy."

Was that what Tosh thought? "I don't hate myself for being gay — not exactly. But I'm afraid I'll hate myself if I give in to temptation, and you'll hate me too. And you hating me isn't something I could bear. I don't want to use you. You mean more to me."

"I won't hate you, I promise. I know you're afraid of the consequences if you come out, but I don't want anyone to stick their noses into our business either, so this works for both of us. No one needs to know."

Sam lurched when Tosh touched his thigh. He had to be honest. He had to tell the truth. Tosh deserved the truth, to make up his own mind, even if they were both careful.

"I can't, Tosh. You don't know the real me. You've no idea about the person I was — am — and what led me here. You deserve more."

Tosh wrapped his hand around the back of his head and pulled him closer. Soft lips touched his own. Sam tasted whiskey. Obviously Tosh had needed Dutch courage before presenting himself. Tosh probed Sam's mouth with his tongue in an effort to gain access, then he stopped with their faces less than an inch apart.

"You want me, don't you?" Tosh cupped Sam's cock now bulging in his jeans.

"Yes," Sam whispered.

"Then why not do this? It's only sex, and we're both grownups. It's not like we'll hate each other in the morning, is it? So I repeat, why not?"

Did Tosh really think this was just sex? Sam pushed away the feeling of hurt those words created. He edged away slightly and straightened, suddenly finding the strength he needed from Tosh's words.

"Because I haven't been completely honest with you."

Tosh touched Sam's arm, re-establishing the connection between them. "It doesn't matter now. We both have pasts."

"Yes, it does." Sam moved Tosh's hand away from him. "It matters because I'm HIV positive."

Chapter Seven

"Shit!" Tosh flinched and moved away immediately.

Sam's heart sank. Tosh grabbed his briefs and a T-shirt and dressed quickly, as if putting a layer of something between them would somehow protect him.

"I'll go," Sam said, rising from the bed.

Tosh stood in front of the bedroom door, effectively blocking him from leaving. "You can't drop a bombshell and leave," he said, placing a hand on Sam's chest.

Sam glanced down. At least Tosh wasn't afraid to touch him. He hoped it was a good sign.

"I don't know what else to do." Sam dug his hands into the pockets of his jeans and stood staring at the carpeted floor until Tosh put a finger under his chin and lifted his head to face him.

"How long have you known?" Tosh asked.

"Over ten years."

"Bloody hell. And you're all right?"

"Can we sit again? I'm shaking so much I'm not sure my legs will hold me."

"Sure, of course. You sit, and I'll go downstairs and make us each a mug of tea. I'd suggest a drink, but I don't want any more. I had a few before you arrived."

Sam sat on the edge of the bed. "I noticed, and tea would be good. My mum always says everything is better after a cup of tea."

"Mine too. I won't be long."

Tosh disappeared through the door and ran down the stairs. Sam tensed then relaxed slowly. He'd done it, and Tosh hadn't told him to go and never darken his door again. He stared around the room. It wasn't the biggest bedroom in the world, but these small houses on the coastal road were basically two up and two downs. He rattled around his house, what he laughingly called The Manse. They'd probably taken space from each bedroom to put in an upstairs bathroom, making them smaller. The walls were painted two different shades of beige, like the carpet, but Tosh had added a blue duvet and curtains. Sam smiled at the collection of *Star Wars* toys on the wide windowsill. If they were originals, they'd be worth a bit of money now that the franchise had been extended again. A large painting filled one wall. Tosh squinted at the signature and was surprised to see it was one of Brice Drummond's landscapes depicting the beach at Cullen. Footsteps echoed on the stairs, and he waited for Tosh to appear, all the while trying to control his erratic breathing and the panic rising in his chest.

Tosh pushed through the door, a mug in each hand. He set them on the bedside cabinet and pulled the chair from the other side of the room to sit facing Sam.

"I'm glad you told me. It took courage to admit your... situation. It can't have been easy. I'm guessing no one in your family knows."

Sam shook his head. "Alec knows I'm gay, but he's the only one, and I haven't told him about my HIV status."

"Shit, Sam. How the hell have you dealt with this and kept it to yourself? I can't even begin to imagine what you've been through. Do the higher-ups in the church know?"

"Officially, the church isn't against gay ministers, and they have my medical records, so I assume they must know. I didn't mention it, and they didn't ask. And there's no danger of me passing on the condition from anything I do in the church. They accepted my vocation when I told them I'd made the choice to be celibate. Since then, the church has moved on and now accepts gay ministers who are married. Except for the HIV label, I'm healthy. I've been lucky with how getting the virus affected me. My viral load is almost undetectable. I eat properly and hardly drink—the wedding was a bit of an exception—and make sure I exercise. These days I take one tablet with my dinner and carry on. I could live a normal life if I'm lucky and careful."

"How did you find out?"

Sam picked up his tea and swallowed a few mouthfuls. Despite the warmth of the night, the sensation of the hot liquid rolling down his throat made him feel more relaxed.

"Interesting question. Most people would want to know how I got it."

"I'm not here to judge you. There but for the grace of God go a lot of us."

"When I first went to university, it was like being a kid let loose in a sweet shop. I slept around and wasn't too careful what I did. I drank a lot and sometimes had sex without using condoms. It was stupid. I'd had enough education to know better, but when you're eighteen, you think you're invincible, or you simply don't think at all. Then I began to feel tired and had flu-like symptoms I couldn't shake. I made an appointment with a doctor and had my blood tested. When they told me, I didn't know what to do. I made up a story and told everyone I had glandular fever. One day, I found myself sitting in a church near the university staring into space, which is where I met Jock. All of it poured out of me and he listened. I discovered he'd founded a center for LGBT kids."

"Is Jock gay?"

"No. It's funny, Alec asked that as well. No, he isn't, but he had a brother who was. His father threw his brother out and he died. His wife, Joyce, is lovely. They took care of me for a while and stopped me from falling apart. I helped at the center, and, after a while, returned to my studies. I decided to become a minister like Jock. I wanted to give something back."

"You could have done that without the God bit," Tosh said.

"True, but I've never regretted my decision. I may not

agree with every word in the Bible—times change. But I prayed, and for me, God listened. I found comfort in the words, and being a part of something greater than myself."

"The church always loves a sinner who repents."

Sam gazed at Tosh. "Yes, it does. I know it's not fashionable to believe, but at least the Church of Scotland has moved on from the past. We've had women ministers since the sixties." He knew he was sounding defensive. "Not every faith can say that much."

"So the church would accept you being in a relationship with another man?"

"They voted on it earlier this year. As long as the local people accept it, then it's possible to appoint someone in a same-sex partnership. I'm not sure what would happen if I decided to come out. I guess the elders would meet in a kirk session and decide whether they wanted me to stay or not. I could move to a city parish where the vote was more in favor. Up here, the vote was close, but still positive." He paused and drank down the rest of his tea, then carefully put the mug down on the cabinet again. "So where does this leave you and me, Tosh?"

"I don't know. It's a lot to take in, and a lot to consider. I'm not going to deny I'm attracted to you but…"

"Me being HIV positive changes things."

"It does, but not because I'm afraid of catching it from you. I know you wouldn't put me in any danger you could avoid. In fact, I read somewhere that it's safer to have sex with someone who knows their status. There are lots of people out there who don't and aren't too careful. You made a mistake. Other people with HIV manage their lives, and I don't imagine I can get it from kissing you or anything stupid like that. But this can't simply be something casual for either of us, not anymore, despite what I said earlier. If we're going to do this, we have to make plans for the what-if situation. Tongues will wag, Sam. You know what it's like around here. Everyone knows I'm gay, and you're single. Having had the odd girlfriend over the years isn't going to protect you from speculation forever. Are you prepared for everything to come out, so to speak?"

"I've decided to tell the rest of my family. Alec says they'd be all right, and I think they would. My parents will probably be less surprised than when I told them I was being ordained." He yawned. "Sorry, confession may be good for the soul, but I'm exhausted and you've got to get up early. I should be getting home now."

Tosh put a hand on his arm. "Don't go. Stay here. Sleep with me—just sleep. I don't know about you, but I could use a cuddle."

Sam nodded. "I'd like that. I need to pay a visit first."

"I'll be here," Tosh said, rising then making his way around the bed.

In the bathroom, Sam stared at his reflection in the mirror, noting his puffy, red-ringed eyes. He rubbed toothpaste on his teeth with his finger then swilled out his mouth. Tosh lay in the bed facing away from him when he returned.

Raising the sheet, having removed his jeans and socks, Sam slipped in behind Tosh. When he lifted his arm to drape it around Tosh's waist, Tosh grabbed him and held it tight. Sam pressed his chest to Tosh's back and breathed in his familiar scent. It comforted him enough to close his eyes. Maybe Tosh would feel differently in the morning light, but for now, he was there and Tosh was in his arms.

* * * *

Tosh enjoyed the summer months. It was easier dealing with a four-thirty alarm call when the sun was already sending out shards of light across the sky. Even so, he reached over and turned the radio off immediately. Sam stirred behind him, and the tell-tale press of a morning boner hard against his arse matched his own. For a few minutes, he contemplated calling in sick, but that wasn't him, and if he had, no doubt his mother would have appeared within hours when he didn't deliver her post.

"Wow, this really is early," Sam said, rubbing his eyes as he stared at the clock. Sam's early-morning croak sounded growly and sexy to Tosh's ears.

"The postman's lot," he replied.

Sam reached an arm around him, as if to stop him moving, and he pushed back. Whether by accident or design, Sam's hand brushed over his erection.

"Would you like a hand dealing with that?" Sam asked.

Would I?

"Let me. Please."

Tosh picked up Sam's hand and placed it on his cock. Sam wrapped his fingers around Tosh's erection and began to move up and down, slowly at first then with more urgency.

"Good," he whispered. "Feels so good." Sam's hand on his cock and the feel of his body against his back proved too much. Tosh came quickly, spilling over Sam's hand into his briefs. He breathed out in an effort to calm his senses as Sam wiped his hand on Tosh's T-shirt.

"What about you?" he asked, conscious of the erection still poking into his back.

"Too complicated. Spontaneity can be a bit of an issue," Sam replied. "I'll survive blue balls. I'm well practiced."

"I have to get ready for work," Tosh said, pulling away. "You stay here if you want. I'll leave you the spare key."

"Can't. I should be gone too. We can't have the local minister being caught doing the walk of shame. There won't be many people in the streets at this time away from the harbor."

"I suppose not. I'm going to have a shower. Do you want to use the loo before me?"

"Yeah, then I'll go down and make us tea before I go."

Fifteen minutes later, Tosh came into the kitchen to find Sam dressed, the washing up done, and two large mugs of tea on the counter.

"I didn't know what you wanted for breakfast."

"I usually grab a couple of cereal bars to eat on my round, and have a large brunch at Maggie's café."

57

"I'll finish this then and get off."

Tosh placed a hand on Sam's arm. "Sam, I think we may have something here, but I don't want to rush, and, even though I don't want to hide, I realize things are so much more complicated for you than they are for me."

"You need proof I'm serious."

"I suppose so. I've never been one for playing the field. Between Darach and Harry, there weren't many, and no one serious—not much opportunity around here, to be honest. When I met Harry, he'd moved up here to get away from too many memories." Tosh swallowed a large gulp of tea. "Harry was ten years my senior, and he'd been in a relationship with an older man himself. His partner died. He was HIV positive as well. So, HIV isn't the bogeyman for me."

Sam's eyes widened with surprise.

"Harry wasn't infected himself, but he told me before we slept together to give me the information I needed. He showed me his test results. He told me some of the stories his partner had told him of HIV and AIDs diagnosis and treatment in the eighties, and those bloody awful adverts they did. So much prejudice and fear, and people being treated like lepers—awful. I'm not saying you being positive isn't an issue, but there are ways to deal with it, and there's this new drug I read about."

"You mean PrEP. I've heard of it, but I wouldn't expect you to take drugs to be with me."

"You have to decide what you want, Sam. This is a big decision for both of us, and you've a lot more to lose than I have. Maybe you should talk to Jock—have a break from here."

"I have to admit, it would be great to see him and Joyce again. I haven't been there for over a year. Thank you. Thank you for not sending me away last night."

"I needed you here as much as you wanted to stay." It was true. He missed being with someone. "Get your head sorted, Sam, and come back to me. I'm not asking you to stand in the pulpit and declare to all and sundry, but I need something."

Sam nodded, swallowed his tea and stood. "I'd better get off now."

Tosh grabbed a hoodie from the back of the sofa. "Here, put this on with the hood up. You being in civvies means fewer people will recognize you."

Sam leaned in and kissed him. "I think you're right about visiting Glasgow. I haven't had a holiday in a while. One of the elders can take the services. I had a good night, Tosh, and morning."

Tosh noticed the use of his nickname again. "I liked it when you called me Brodie, even if you're the only one other than my mother, and half the time she forgets and calls me Tosh as well."

"I'll ring you from Glasgow."

Tosh leaned in and wrapped his arms around Sam, kissing him under his ear. Sam returned his hug then opened his front door and glanced both ways. "The coast is clear if you go now."

Sam pulled up the hood and scurried to his car, jumped in and set off. Only time would tell whether Sam was ready to change his life in such a huge way. Tosh grabbed his jacket from the hook and locked the door behind him, trying to ignore his own lingering question of whether *he* was also ready to move on from the past.

Chapter Eight

Glasgow. It was hard to believe ten years had passed since he'd lived there. He strolled from the station to the center, gazing at the architecture and in the shop windows. As he walked, he noted how even the air tasted different. Where he lived now had none of the noise, high buildings or traffic. Glasgow was busy with people shopping and working. He hoped he'd be able to get in a visit to the new science center as well as the Botanical Gardens. He'd always found it peaceful to sit among the plants.

As was typical of Scotland, after a few warmer days, which would likely constitute Scotland's summer, the weather had taken a turn for the worse. A chill wind blew down the street behind him and the dark gray sky threatened rain. He pulled his jacket around him and strode out.

Somehow, many years ago, Jock had persuaded the local council to let him have an old civic building which was no longer needed. Through his contacts, Jock had organized people who would help with education and skills development as well as medical care and emotional support. The statistics on young people thrown out of their homes when they came out were frightening, as was what could happen to them on the streets. To Sam, Jock and his wife were saints.

When he arrived outside the building, Sam didn't enter straight away. A young man hovered on the steps, staring up at the door. He danced from one foot to the other with his arms wrapped around his body, as if he was unsure what to do.

"Do you want to go in?" Sam asked.

The teenager stared at him, all eyes and pinched cheeks.

"You look as if you haven't eaten in a while. Why don't you come in with me and we can find you something to eat? My name is Sam. A long time ago Jock and Joyce helped me out too."

The boy nodded. Sam guessed he was sixteen, but he could have been any age. "Let's go in then, shall we?"

Once through the door, Sam listened for noise. The sound of conversation came from the big room on the left. Through the glass door, Sam saw several people sitting at tables and he smelled breakfast.

"Hmm, there's bacon this morning." He held the door open and let the boy enter under his arm. At the far end, Joyce stood doling out bacon sarnies. His own mouth watered. "Sit a minute, and I'll let them know you're here. You're safe now. I promise."

When Joyce saw him, she greeted him with a huge smile. "Sam, laddie, it's so good to see you again. You're as handsome as ever, I see."

Heat flushed his cheeks. Joyce always had the same effect, claiming that was what mothers were for. And although he'd had his own mother, Joyce knew the truth of his circumstances so there was no distance between them. A pang of guilt caused his heart to sink for a moment, but there was no time to feel sad when he was being hugged by a five-foot-three bundle of Glaswegian dynamite.

"It's good to see you, Joyce. It's been too long."

"It has, laddie. Jock will be so happy to see you again. He's at the cash and carry this morning, but he'll be back soon."

"Any chance of one of those sarnies? I left early this morning and I'm famished. I also found the young man over there on the doorstep. I'll take one over to him and get his story, shall I?"

"David is around somewhere. He's our new volunteer helping us out during the summer holidays. He's studying for his PhD, and he's rather handsome."

Sam stared at her. "Joyce Baird, you are incorrigible. Anyone would think you were trying to set me up."

"Maybe, but he is a lovely man, much like yourself. I'll finish up here and go find him, then we can see how we can help this young lad you've found."

Sam picked up the sandwiches and a couple of coffees and made his way back to where the boy sat. He practically pounced on the food, biting and swallowing quickly.

"Take your time," Sam said. "There's more where that came from. Joyce will finish serving breakfast and get someone to talk to you about how they can help you here, but for now, you have me."

The boy ate the rest of the sandwich more slowly, then wiped his mouth with his sleeve and swallowed a few mouthfuls of coffee while Sam waited. In his experience, there was no point in rushing someone.

Finally, he glanced away from the food and table and at Sam. "My name is Ryan. I've just turned sixteen and I'm from a small village in Caithness. My Dad chucked me out a month ago. I came here to find work, but I've run out of money. The weather has been good until today, so I've slept rough for a few nights in different parks. Someone told me to try here, that the people were good, and they'd help me find a job and a place to stay. Last night, there was a man, but I didn't want to... I mean, I haven't before... Only fooled around."

"It's all right. You'll be safe here. It must have been hard for you—what your Dad did?"

Ryan nodded. "He found stuff on my computer, photographs of men."

Sam allowed himself a small smile. "I get the picture."

"He yelled at me. Said no son of his could be a fairy."

"Did he hit you?"

"No, but he was so angry. I've always known he had a temper, but I thought it wouldn't matter, that even though he'd made comments in the past, I was his son so it would be different."

"But it did matter?" Sam questioned.

"He told me to choose. But how could I? How could I agree to be what I'm not? What was I supposed to do? Find a girl, get married and learn to fix motors like he does? I've no interest in engines."

"Do you have any idea what you want to do?"

"You're going to think I'm mad."

"Try me."

"I want to work on a cruise liner. I don't mind what I do. I want to see other parts of the world. My village has around five hundred people who live in each other's pockets, knowing each other's business. I want to meet lots of people. There must be loads of jobs on those massive liners."

Sam witnessed Ryan's first smile and the flush of excitement in his cheeks. He knew what it was to grow up in a small community where everyone knew your name and generations of your family history—where *he* was simply one of the Carmichael boys. His desire to be different had brought him to Glasgow, but he'd chosen to be pulled back into the fold, and into the closet. This sixteen-year-old boy had more guts than he did. Sam jumped at the touch of a hand on his shoulder and turned.

"Sam, this is David. I've filled him in with a few snippets of information."

Warmth spread up Sam's neck to his cheeks. Joyce hadn't been wrong, David was handsome in a rugged, outdoorsy sort of way with his plaid shirt, blue jeans and huge boots. Glancing up, Sam noted the wide shoulders and cool blue eyes currently scrutinizing him.

David held out a hand. "It's good to meet you, Reverend."

Sam glanced at Ryan, catching the look of surprise in his eyes. "Please, call me Sam. Here, I'm another one of Jock and Joyce's willing victims—sorry, helpers. It's good to meet you, David."

The handshake was firm, the hand dry and David's smile wide and genuine.

"This is Ryan," Sam said. "He's been telling me about himself and how he'd love to work on a cruise liner. I thought Jock might have some contacts."

Joyce smiled. "You know my husband. There's always someone. Right, son, why don't you let David show you around while I get the kitchen sorted? Jock should be back soon with supplies."

Ryan straightened up at Joyce's words. "Thank you. I don't have any money, but I'd be happy to help in the kitchen or anything."

"We'll see, laddie." Joyce patted his arm. "Now off you go. You picked the right day to arrive as we've a vacancy."

Sam stood and waited while David led Ryan up the wide staircase. "Do you really have a free bed, or have you shoved one into a room for him?"

"You know us, Sam. We always find space for them somehow. This one needs feeding up. I'd guess he hasn't eaten much recently. He's skin and bones. Now, what about you? Fancy giving me a hand in the kitchen, and you can fill me in on why you're here? From what Jock told me, which wasn't much, you've something on your mind."

Sam nodded and followed her into the kitchen.

"I'll wash and you wipe, and off you go, then. Tell Aunty Joyce."

Sam filled her in on the details of his current predicament as well as Tosh. Here and there, Joyce would ask a question, but mostly she ummed and ahhed.

"So what do I do? If I want a relationship with Brodie, I'm going to have to risk everything—my job *and* my family. I don't think my parents will have a problem, but my congregation is full of older people. I've brought in a younger group, but you know what it's like in everyday parishes. It's not like working with students."

A door creaked open and the clunking sound of heavy boots striding across the dining room floor made them turn. A large body pushed forcefully through the swing doors.

"Ah, Sam, you're here. Come and give a poor old man a

hand bringing the stuff in, will you?"

Sam hugged his old mentor. "It's good to see you, and don't lie. You're as fit as a fiddle."

A couple of boys appeared at the bottom of the stairs and made to turn around.

"Rory, Jamie, get here and help us. I've news for both of you," Jock commanded.

The boys shrugged but turned around anyway and stomped down the stairs.

"Right, this shouldn't take us long." Sam helped carry bags of supplies into the kitchen then waited while Jock talked to the boys.

"Rory, I've found a place for you to train as a mechanic. You'll have to go to college as well, but the owner will be expecting you tomorrow. I'll give you the details later. Jason, I've checked on the course you wanted and pulled a few strings. You'll be baking before you know it. You can help Joyce and practice here as well. Homemade bread will be lovely."

Sam's heart expanded, seeing the shy smiles on both boys' faces. He knew for Josh such smiles would be thanks enough. They would have somewhere to live, and an opportunity to work, and, although it might not be luxurious, it was safe and clean.

Sam helped them put everything away and joined Jock in the dining room.

"So, Sammy." Jock was the one person who ever called him that. "How long can you stay? It's so good to see you again."

Sam smiled. "Only a few days, I'm afraid. You know what it's like. When was the last time you and Joyce had a holiday?"

"We had a weekend in Edinburgh last year. It's difficult to find someone to take care of this place, but we've a few new volunteers, so we might manage another weekend."

"Yes, Joyce introduced me to David earlier."

Jock gave one of his deep, throaty chuckles. "Did she say

how handsome he is?"

"She did."

"She worries that you're lonely and won't let people near you."

"I told her about me and Brodie. I don't know what to do."

"It depends on how strongly you feel, but I'll be honest here, laddie. You shouldn't even consider coming out if you're not doing it for yourself. If you're thinking of doing it as a declaration of the extent of your love for him, then don't. This decision should be about you and what you're comfortable with. We both know the Church has moved on, but many of the folk who turn up to worship haven't. You made the decision not to come out all those years ago, and I supported your choice."

"Against your better judgment."

"Yes, that's as maybe. I know you didn't want to make waves."

"But you think I was wrong."

"Sam, I can't tell you how to live your life. Only you can do that. Ask yourself, is it time?"

"I want to tell my parents and my family. Alec, my eldest brother knows. I've always hated lying to them."

"And the HIV?"

"I'll tell them about my status as well."

"Do you love this Brodie?"

"I don't know. I've never been in love. It's more than a physical thing between us, but it's complicated."

Jock laughed again. "Isn't it always?"

"Brodie is a widower. His husband was murdered. You must have read it in the papers—the Brice Drummond kidnapping and attempted murder?"

"Yes—a bad business. If I remember, his husband acted bravely in trying to stop the gang."

"Yes, he did. It's been over a year, but what if I come out to everyone and I'm just a rebound experiment for him?"

"Ah, laddie. You've got your knickers in a twist

overthinking this, haven't you? Ask yourself what's the worst that could happen."

"I could lose my job *and* Brodie."

"Without intending to be too blunt—there are other jobs and other men. Have you seen the vacancies list recently? Lots of parishes needing ministers, including a few in Glasgow. Your sexuality and status would matter less here, and you'd have lots to do."

"You make it sound so simple, but then you always did. Practical Christianity was always your strength. I hope you can help the boy I found on the doorstep this morning."

"I haven't met him yet. Joyce left him with David. We'll have a chat later."

"He wants to work on a cruise liner and see the world."

"It's a happy coincidence my brother is a quartermaster, then. The boy might be in luck. Do you have any plans for this afternoon?"

"I thought I might have a wander around, visit the new science center, maybe pop into the university while it's quiet."

"Then we'll see you at our house for dinner this evening. I hope you've kept up your Scrabble skills. Joyce can't wait to play."

* * * *

As Sam strolled around the city, he mulled over what Jock had said. He was right, of course. He needed to tell the truth for himself, not for others. Brodie hadn't demanded he declare himself as part of the deal, but he didn't want to see him in secret, and all it would take was for someone to see him sneaking out of Brodie's house in the wee small hours of the morning. The fishermen rose early around their way, and everyone knew everyone else's business.

Sitting on the steps overlooking the river as they ate a sandwich for lunch, two young men sat closely together, touching each other, feeding each other bits of cake. The shy glances and smiles told him they were more than friends, but maybe it was still early days in their relationship. No one else showed any interest at all. No one pointed at them or called them names. There was the odd nudge, perhaps, but nothing overt. Sam glanced the other way. There, two older ladies were sitting on a bench, chatting. Were they a couple too? Could he have that? Could he and Brodie grow old together? Did he want such a future, and how much was he prepared to give up?

He brushed the crumbs from his jeans and smiled as a sparrow darted across then picked them up. Standing, he made a decision. He would tell his family. It wouldn't be easy, but Alec and Sandie were already on his side. He also wanted to talk to Jock about another idea he had. If anyone knew how to set up a youth group, they did. He wanted to do something in his area, not just for LGBT youth but for all the bored teenagers. He could get Gus on board, as he had contacts at the school. Happy he'd made two decisions, he strode up the concrete steps and read the instructions on how to get to the science center. His phone pinged and he removed it from his pocket.

I hope you're having a good time. I've had an interesting day.

Brodie. He messaged back.

Yes, Jock and Joyce are well and I've a lot to think about. I'll explain when I return. Good interesting or bad interesting? Sam pressed send.

Good interesting. Looking forward to seeing you.

Sam wasn't sure if he was entirely comfortable with his decision, but it was time to face the music.

Chapter Nine

The meet-up in the car park of the motel had been awkward. It had been Jock's idea to ask Tosh to meet him halfway so they could talk with the anonymity of being somewhere where no one knew them. At least in this sort of motel they could sleep together, or separately. Sam wasn't taking anything for granted. He had no right to expect anything.

Now, at Sam's suggestion, they occupied a table in the corner of the pub attached to the motel. It shouldn't be called a pub, really. Like all of these places, the furniture, décor and food were standard, but midweek it was full of businessmen glued to their laptops or other technology. Sam ordered their food at the bar and returned with drinks, taking the seat adjacent to Tosh so they didn't have to speak too loudly to hear each other.

"I couldn't believe it when you told me what had happened. I bet you didn't expect you'd be helping Susie McDougall give birth." Sam was grateful they had something neutral to talk about to break the ice between them.

"I spent most of the time scared witless. At least Susie knew what she was doing, and her other two were at playgroup to give her a rest. When I got there to deliver a couple of parcels, I heard shouting coming from the kitchen. She was on the floor in a pool of water, clutching her stomach. I don't know how women do it. Whoever called them the weaker sex wants their head read. I tell you, it gave me a whole new respect for both our mothers. Mine nearly died giving birth to me, and yours had five huge boys."

"You were saying," Sam said.

"Oh, yes. I phoned for an ambulance and tried to get hold of Donny, but there was no signal. He was harvesting the far fields, so it was only her and me. First time I've ever removed a woman's knickers."

Sam smiled. Tosh's smirk and shining eyes made his stomach flutter in a good way.

"I remembered they always say to get towels and hot water, though I'd no idea what for. Then Susie began to scream the baby was coming. I mean, I'd seen the films in school, and watched episodes of *Call the Midwife,* but nothing prepares you for the sight of a bloody head emerging from between a woman's legs while she calls her husband all the names under the sun."

Sam turned at the chuckle behind him to find the waiter standing with their starters. He placed them in front of them and moved away easily between the tables.

"You were checking out his arse?" Tosh asked.

"I might have been," Sam replied, heat rushing to his cheeks.

"Me too. Anyway, I see the head crowning then the shoulders and all of a sudden there she is, bloody and beautiful with a shock of red hair. Susie told me to leave the cord attached for now and wait for the placenta. And believe me, that isn't pretty. They don't show you the graphic details on the telly."

"Some women eat them, I'm told, or even leave them attached to the baby for days. I was at home with Mum one night and this program came on showing three women giving birth. Mum told me that we came out quickly with no problems. She pulled a face when one of them ate the placenta."

"I'm not surprised. So, I wrapped up the baby and put her on Susie and soon after Ellis McKenzie arrived. Everything was fine, so they called off the ambulance, and I hurried to fetch Donny. He sounded relieved to have missed it all."

"How was the dark and brooding doctor?"

"He's a changed man since he became a dad himself—

much less grumpy. By the time we returned, mother and baby were tidied up and Susie was breastfeeding on the sofa in the living room. I still had my round to finish off. They're going to name the baby after me, you know. Matilda Brodie McDougall, and Susie's asked me to be godparent. That'll definitely be the full set for us—a wedding, funeral and a baptism."

"Poor girl getting lumbered with your name. Still they could have called her Tosh, and you know what Tosh means?"

"Of course I do, but with my surname, being nicknamed Tosh was inevitable."

The main courses arrived.

"So, you haven't said much about your trip to Glasgow."

Sam chewed his smothered chicken then swallowed, giving himself time. "It was great to see Jock and Joyce again. They're so dedicated. I met a young lad on the doorstep when I arrived at the center. He appeared terrified and looked so young. His father had chucked him out. I still find it hard to believe a parent would behave in such a way, but his did. I've decided to set up a youth club back home in the town. The kids have nowhere to go, and that's what gets them into trouble. I thought Gus and Darach might help, considering their school contacts. I have the community center we could use, and I'm sure a few of the churchgoers would volunteer. I thought I'd go to the school myself and see what the kids want. No point in setting something up if they're not interested."

"I'd be happy to help if you want me."

Sam couldn't help himself. "I want you." Tosh gazed at him wide-eyed for a moment. Sam placed his hand on Tosh's arm. "I know it's complicated."

"I'm not totally ignorant of the problems. I've done research, you know—about sex." He lowered his voice on the last word and glanced around.

Despite the seriousness of the conversation, Sam found he wanted to laugh. They were like two of those old women mouthing certain words when they talked to each other over a wall.

"Have you?"

"Yes, and there are activities we can indulge in as long as we are careful. I brought supplies with me."

"Me too," Sam said. "I didn't want to take anything for granted but..."

"I think we both knew we weren't meeting here for nothing." Tosh lifted his hand and signaled to the waiter for the bill.

Ten minutes later, Sam was sitting on the bed opposite Tosh, who sat on the bed settee.

"Now we're alone, care to share what else you decided on your trip?"

Sam stared down at his hands clasped together in his lap. He needed to make eye contact with Tosh. He lifted his head and met Tosh's gaze. "I'm going to tell my family I'm gay."

"And HIV positive?"

"I don't know. I wondered if both was too much."

"Or you could get it over with in one go."

"True. They should know everything. I've decided to ask Mum and Dad to have us over for Sunday lunch after church. Hamish won't be there, but the others can be. I don't want to have to tell them in dribs and drabs. As for Granny, I'll have to tackle that one another time, or not at all."

"Sounds sensible. Do you intend to tell them about us?"

"Is there an us?" Sam asked.

"I'd be lying if I said I didn't have any interest in there being an us. And if you tell your family, it's a start. I understand if you want to keep it from the church, but you know it'll come out eventually. We live in a small place and everyone knows I'm gay. If I hadn't been mourning Harry, and you weren't the local minister, I expect tongues would have been wagging already."

"About Harry. Are you sure you're ready to move on?"

Tosh placed a hand on his arm. "I've thought about this,

you know. I'm not a casual sort of man. I loved Harry. Part of me will always love him but he would be the first to tell me life goes on. If you're worried about being a rebound shag, stop. Let's face it. If I wanted a quick fuck, I wouldn't be here with you."

"I suppose not. I'm just a bit nervous about what this all means for both of us."

"Stop overthinking things. Let's go to bed and see what happens, shall we?"

Sam covered Tosh's hand with his own and squeezed. "I'd like that. This bed feels so comfortable and is big enough for three. We wouldn't even have to touch each other."

Tosh stood and made his way around the bed to the bathroom. "I don't know how I don't touch you whenever you're near enough. Believe me, in bed we'll be touching."

Sam shivered at the thought and began to undress as soon as Tosh closed the bathroom door.

Even though they'd already slept in the same bed, Sam, conscious of wearing only his briefs, hurried across the room to use the bathroom while Tosh watched intently from under the duvet. Cleaning his teeth, he stared at his reflection in the mirror. It had been so long since he'd had a relationship with someone. His longest boyfriend had lasted three months in his final year of university, but the guilt of knowing he'd intended to train for the ministry had overwhelmed him and soured any chance he'd had to continue. Much had changed in the last ten years, but he still had doubts, despite the recent decisions to accept gay ministers in civil partnerships. Most congregations were full of older people, not that it meant they were all prejudiced… Now he was tying himself in knots overthinking everything. All he wanted to concentrate on at the moment was the man waiting for him in the bed.

Sam was happy enough in his own skin to appreciate his own good looks. He'd had enough people show interest in him over the years. Many had said he was lucky not to get the family's ginger hair and freckles, although he did have a smattering across his shoulders from being out in the sun when it occasionally deigned to shine in Scotland. Brodie wasn't lean or tall. He had no six-pack hidden under his clothes and Sam liked Brodie's softness and his slightly receding hairline. It made him more human. Then there were his calves and thighs, strong from the walking he did. A sudden vision of those thighs wrapped around him as he drove into Brodie's arse appeared from nowhere. Would they get to such a stage? Would he let him? Maybe some time in the future, but not tonight. He swilled the toothpaste from his mouth, sure he had no cuts in there, and gave his hands a quick check as well, then opened the door.

Tosh lay with his hands behind his head, trying to appear casual when he was anything but. This was a big deal for him. He'd done his research and knew the dangers, but he also knew Sam wouldn't take any chances.

He pulled back the duvet and, after a moment's hesitation, Sam climbed in beside him and turned to face him. Tosh smiled, hoping it would dispel both his and Sam's nerves, then leaned in and kissed Sam. Tosh opened his mouth, but didn't push in with his tongue, although he moved close enough for their bodies to touch. Despite his nervousness, Tosh was already semi-hard while Sam's erection pushed against his thigh. He broke off the kiss and moved down, pressing kisses along Sam's collar bone and down his chest until he licked around a nipple. Sam groaned and arched toward him.

"Feels good," he muttered.

Tosh glanced upward before moving across to the other nipple and circling one while squeezing the other gently with his fingers. Sam rubbed himself against Tosh's thigh.

Lifting his head, Tosh met Sam's eyes staring down at him. Tosh longed to take Sam into his mouth and taste him, but Sam would undoubtedly insist on erring on the side of caution. Instead, he rolled back and removed a condom and lube from the bedside table.

"I want to suck you off," he said simply.

"You don't have to," Sam said. "I can touch myself and you can watch. Having you here and not being by myself is enough."

Tosh opened the wrapper and removed the condom with shaking hands. "No, if we use this and enough lube it will be fine. Even if I can't taste you, I want to feel the weight of you on my tongue and the size of you stretching my lips. I bought strawberry-flavored lube. It'll be fine. Neither of us will be careless, but I don't want you to worry, either. I'm a grown man, Sam, and I make my own decisions. I want to be here with you. And, even though my common sense thinks I've lost the plot, I don't care."

"You should care."

"Okay, maybe I used the wrong words, but with your viral load undetectable I'm not in much danger. I know what's lurking in those shorts and I want it on my tongue."

The corners of Sam's mouth turned upward as he attempted a smile. Tosh lowered the waistband of Sam's briefs and pulled his cock free of the cotton material. Before he encased the swollen flesh in rubber, Tosh lay with his head on Sam's stomach and pushed his impressive cock, grinning when it bounced back. Sam was long but not too wide. He traced a vein along its full length with a single finger, then cupped Sam's balls with one hand. Tosh slipped the rubber over Sam's erection then slathered the shaft with lube. The scent of strawberry filled the air, somewhat artificial but near enough to the real thing. Tosh blamed his mother's craving for strawberries while pregnant for his love of the soft fruit. He clasped Sam's cock in his hand then stroked up and down, sliding slowly while Sam leaned back on his elbows, watching.

"All right?" Tosh asked, moving his jaw to stop grinding his teeth.

"Yeah," Sam replied, his breath coming in pants. "Don't stop."

Tosh kept stroking for a while before moving his other

hand to squeeze Sam's balls again and roll them one at a time across his palm. After a few minutes, he positioned himself so he could take the tip of Sam's cock in his mouth. The combination of lube and rubber wasn't the most pleasant, but he sucked enough to make Sam arch up, pushing himself farther into Tosh's mouth. Tosh kept moving his hand until Sam's balls drew up. He wasn't sure whether to keep sucking or to stroke Sam to his orgasm. In the end, he decided he wanted to watch Sam's face when he came and turned his gaze upward. Sam had his mouth open, breathing hard, and a look of concentration on his face with his neck arched backward. Tosh increased his speed until Sam, moaning loudly, came into the condom. For a few moments, Tosh lay there, unsure of what to do, waiting for Sam to regain his composure.

Finally, Sam sat up and removed the condom, tying it off and placing it in a bag on his side of the bed. Having tucked himself back into his briefs, he turned to face Tosh. For a few seconds, neither of them spoke and Tosh hoped this wasn't going to be awkward. There was also the matter of his own erection currently threatening to fade away.

"Thank you," Sam said. "Thank you for trusting me. With everything in my life, I know you're taking a chance here." Sam took a deep breath, and Tosh wondered what was coming next.

"I want to ask you to do something."

"O-kay."

"I've no idea if you're a bottom or a top. I've done both. It's less dangerous for you to fuck me —"

Tosh breathed in sharply. "I don't know if…if I'm ready."

Sam placed a hand on Tosh's chest. "It's all right. I'm not asking you to fuck me now, but you could slip your cock between my thighs from behind, you know. I need… I want… to connect, to feel you against me and this is the nearest we can get."

Tosh breathed out again. He could do that. Sometimes, in the early morning, he and Harry had done it if they couldn't be bothered to prep one another. "Turn over," he whispered. Shit, the man was perfect. He ran a finger over Sam's arse then up his back to the nape of his neck. Sam shivered under his touch. Tosh peppered him just below the hairline with tiny kisses.

"Oh, God, I love that. Don't stop."

"You taste so good," Tosh murmured. "Need more." He pressed his lips over Sam's shoulders and upper body before finally moving down his spine, noting the freckles. "I see you didn't entirely escape the sign of the ginger, then. I'd kiss each one, but there are quite a few. Lift your leg."

Tosh covered himself with lube and slipped his cock between Sam's thighs, shifting his chest against Sam's spine and wrapping his arm around Sam to connect hand in hand. Tosh pushed forward then drew back, keeping up the movement, enjoying the warmth and the friction. He knew it wouldn't take long and concentrated on the feelings. It wasn't the same as plunging into a tight arse, but it was near enough not to matter now. All he needed was to feel close to Sam, to know neither of them were alone and they had each other to hold on to.

A familiar tingling sensation danced down his spine and he stiffened in preparation for release. He clutched Sam's hand tighter and laid his forehead on Sam's shoulder. He breathed in the scent of Sam's cologne and shampoo, as well as the sweat caused by the warmth of the evening and their closeness. He came with a shout, releasing streams of liquid between Sam's thighs as he deliberately tightened around Tosh. They'd need to clean Sam off, or he'd wake with his legs stuck together.

Tosh rolled over and gasped for air, his chest rising and falling until he regained his equilibrium. Sam jumped out of the bed, returned with a towel from his bag and began to clean himself then Tosh, before settling down with his head on Tosh's chest.

"Was that all right?" he asked.

Tosh could see the uncertainty and worry in Sam's

expression. He leaned over and kissed him, gently sucking on his lower lip. "It was perfect," he said. And it had been. He didn't need to lie. "I'm tired now. Let's sleep, and tomorrow we can drive somewhere for lunch, even if we are in separate cars, before we have to return home."

"No regrets?" Sam asked, staring at him.

"No regrets," Tosh said. "I wanted this too."

"I *will* tell them, Tosh. It's time they knew the truth—about everything."

Tosh lifted the strand of blond hair that had fallen over Sam's forehead and cupped his cheek, running his fingers through the soft hair of his beard. Now that he was getting used to it, Tosh had begun to enjoy the sensation when they kissed. He raised himself onto one elbow and moved his hand to stroke Sam's chest. "Just make sure you're telling them for the right reasons. Remember you're doing this for you. Whatever we may have together, you have to do this for yourself, not for me. I didn't expect to feel this way about anyone again, especially not so soon after...but I care for you, Sam Carmichael, despite telling myself not to. Whatever you decide, I'm here to support you, remember that, will you? Your family love you, and I'm sure they'll be fine with what you tell them."

"Thank you. It means a lot to me. I know I'm going to hurt them. I won't be the person they think I am anymore, and it'll take time."

"Come on, there'll be enough time for such angst in the future. Turn over and let me tuck in behind you."

Tosh closed his eyes, breathing in the smell of the man in front of him. His coming out to his Catholic mother had been hard enough, but he couldn't imagine what it would be like to reveal such a secret to a close-knit family like the Carmichaels. He listened until Sam's breathing steadied then let himself drift off to sleep.

Chapter Ten

Sam had performed a christening at the morning service in the small village church he also ministered to so he was running late. Tosh didn't join him on these occasions, but they'd spoken the night before, a conversation that had ended in rather satisfying phone sex.

"Do you want me to lock up for you, Reverend?"

Sam was abruptly pulled away from the memory by the voice of the church elder.

"Thank you, Mrs. McPherson. I'm away to my parents' for Sunday lunch with the family, and I'm already running late."

"You get along there, then. Your mother will be cross if the dinner is ruined. I'll sort out here. It was wonderful to see so many people here today, and they got to listen to your sermon. I've always been a particular believer in not casting the first stone. Too many people are ready to judge others at the drop of a hat. Look at those reality programs and people hiding behind the anonymity of the Internet. A lot of it seems to consist of downright bullying as far as I can tell."

Sam stared at the woman in front of him. With her gray hair formed into a bun, and her tweed skirt and jacket, she represented everyone's stereotypical image of an older, widowed, female church elder set in her ways and steeped in the past.

"I'm glad you enjoyed my words, Mrs. McPherson. Do unto others as you would have them do to you has always been a particular favorite of mine too. And now I must be away. Thank you for locking up."

On the drive to his parents' house, he considered Mrs. McPherson's words and realized he'd been as guilty as anyone in judging her. As an elder, she had a large say in the doings of the church and must have chosen him for the position. Her husband had died a few years back. He'd been much more the fire-and-brimstone type of believer, and absolutely outraged over many of the church reforms. He'd never have accepted a gay minister, let alone one with HIV. He gripped the wheel harder in an effort to control his nerves. He hoped Tosh was right with his assumption that his family would be supportive.

When he arrived, there were already several cars parked within the drive of the single-story croft his parents had moved to when his father had semi-retired. They'd chosen a beautiful spot up at the top of the village. The old croft had a pretty garden at the back and a view of the Moray Firth. The new conservatory allowed them to watch the changing seasons, the beautiful sunsets and the seabirds as they swooped over the waves, as well as keeping an eye on the grandchildren as they ran around. They'd even seen dolphins playing in the waters on more than one occasion.

"Sorry I'm late," he shouted, entering through the front door. He found his mother in the kitchen and kissed her cheek. "We had the McCleod christening this morning."

"Everyone is already here and in the main room. Dinner will be ready in a few minutes. Tell your father to come and get the knife for this beef. You know he doesn't like anyone else to do it, even your brother."

"I'll tell him, Mum." He pulled his mother into a hug then let her go.

"What was that for?" she asked.

"Do I need a reason to hug my mother? I'll get them up to the table. Do you want help serving?"

"I'll help," Sandie said from behind him. "You take the knife through."

Sam picked up the blade and crossed the small corridor to the main room. It had been knocked through to form a dining area at one end, and when he entered, everyone was already sitting at the large oak table. His father, as always, occupied one of the chairs at the far end. Every face lifted to gaze at him.

He gave the knife to his father and kissed the top of his head before taking his position. On either side of his father sat his brothers, Alec and Stuart, with their wives next to them. The children were dotted around between the adults, with Jenny in her highchair between himself and Sandie. He tickled her under the chin and she giggled. Opposite him sat his youngest brother, Gus, and his new wife, Mel. His mother would take the other c seat at the end of the table.

The joint of beef was placed in front of his father ready for him to carve. Sandie brought in the bowls of vegetables, Yorkshire puddings and a huge gravy boat. Sam sniffed the air with its delicious flavors. Eventually, everyone, including his mother, were seated. His father dished out slices of meat and they tucked in. Conversation centered on the children and the various businesses. Gus regaled them with aspects of the cases he'd had to deal with, and mentioned Darach McNaughton a few times. Was he imagining the frown on his brother Stuart's face every time Gus mentioned Darach? As time passed, his uneasiness increased, and he found it harder to swallow and eat any more. He caught his mother's concerned glance when he placed his cutlery on the plate.

"There's more if you want it, Sam," she said.

"I'm fine, Mum. And I want to leave room for pudding."

"Your mother's made her famous rhubarb and apple pie, laddie, so you'll need room for her pastry."

It was the family's standing joke that his mother's pastry could be rather heavy. Of course it was nothing of the sort.

"So none for you then, Gordon," she said, grinning. "Ellis McKenzie said you had to cut down on your fat intake anyway."

"Och, get away with you, woman. What does he know

anyway? Bloody doctors think they're God half the time. I'm not giving up red meat on that thin bugger's say-so. Anyway, the pie can be one of my five a day."

The rest of them laughed.

When they'd finished eating, everyone found a seat in the living room except Aisling, Stuart's wife, who'd taken the older children out to the garden to run around. Jenny remained, sitting on the floor, making towers with her bricks. Sam inhaled then exhaled in an effort to control his nerves. Sandie put a hand on his arm and leaned toward him.

"Are you okay? You haven't said much today."

It was now or never. He hit the side of his mug with his spoon and all heads turned to stare at him. "I'm glad everyone is here. There's something I have to tell you. It's not going to be the easiest thing to say, or for you to hear, but I'd like to get it out without interruption, please." He caught the knowing glance between Alec and Sandie, and his brother's encouraging smile.

Most of him wanted to curl up and disappear, or sink through the floorboards as everyone stared at him, waiting.

"There's something I've always realized, but I've never known how to tell you. I should have told you years ago, but it was easier not to."

"For God's sake, bro, get on with it."

"Stuart, be quiet, your brother's talking."

His brother frowned again at his mother's admonition.

"All right, this is the basic fact—I'm gay." He waited for the questions, but instead, he was met with a wall of silence and confused glances as everyone in the room gazed at each other. His father broke the silence.

"You're a homosexual?" he questioned. "But you're a minister."

"Yes, Dad. You can be both in this day and age."

"They know?"

"I suppose so. Not officially about me being gay, but there's something else I have to tell you."

"More than the fact you're a poof."

"Stuart, for heaven's sake. How old are you?" Alec gave one of his 'I'm the eldest' glares to his younger brother.

"You knew, didn't you?" Stuart replied. "I can see it on your face. You weren't surprised."

"Yes, I found out for certain a few months ago, but I've always had my suspicions, and calling him names won't help."

"You said there was something else, son." His mother's quiet, worried tone cut through the conversation, and Sam was conscious she hadn't said anything so far. "Have you met someone? Is that why you've decided to tell us now?"

"There is someone, Mum, but it's early days, and we're not going to come out into the open yet. It's complicated."

"So what is the something else, then?" His youngest brother, Gus, had remained silent until then.

Sam swallowed hard and offered up a small prayer. At least he'd had practice explaining this to Tosh. "I knew I was gay before I applied to university, but there weren't a lot of opportunities to meet like-minded people up here." He thought of Darach. "Anyway, I threw myself into everything, and I wasn't too careful."

His mother whispered, "Oh, God," from one side of him. He sat on his shaking hands.

"Remember when I was ill for a while during the first year? I told you I had glandular fever, but I didn't. I had no idea how to tell you. I'm sorry. When I was in hospital, I had all sort of tests." He hesitated. *Don't bottle it now.* "I found out I'm HIV positive, but don't worry, I'm all right. It's under control."

He turned at his mother's gasp as she covered her mouth with her hand, tears already forming at his words. Stuart thumped the arm of the sofa.

"Shit! And I've let you near my boys. He's kissed our kids, Alec. He's endangered them all. You selfish bastard. How could you be so irresponsible?"

Alec frowned. "You should have told us, Sam." Sam

couldn't bear the look of hurt on Alec's and Sandie's faces. He glanced down at Jenny, who had been disturbed from her play by the loud voices.

"I would never put any of you in danger," he said, willing one of his parents to speak.

"You can't possibly be so certain," Stuart continued.

"Yes, I can. My viral load is almost non-existent, and the medication I take keeps everything under control. I could live as long as you. HIV isn't a death sentence today."

His mother's shaking voice interrupted them. "What about all those awful adverts from the eighties with the icebergs. Why weren't you more careful? Did someone force you, or deliberately infect you?"

"I don't think so, Mum. Not everyone knows their status. I was young and stupid, and had too much to drink on occasion, but I'm fine, honestly."

His father wrapped his arms around his wife as she sat on the arm of his chair and pulled her close. "This other person — does he know?"

"Yes, Dad, he knows."

"Sod this. I can't believe you're sitting around behaving as if this is nothing. Dad, you must have something to say." Stuart stood, his face red with anger.

"Sit down son. We've had a shock. I won't have such language used in front of the children."

"But you don't care how he's put them in danger." His raised voice brought Aisling and the four boys back into the room.

"I heard the shouting. What's going on?" she asked, sitting on a chair and wrapping her arms around each of her boys while the other two went to Sandie.

Stuart crossed his arms. "My brother has announced he's a queer and infected with HIV like it's nothing and we should accept it and move on, and no one but me appears to be bothered that he's been around our children. God knows what else he's riddled with."

"I'm sorry everyone. I'll leave." Sam made a move to get

up.

Aisling clutched his sleeve, pulling him back down. "No, Sam. Sit down. I'm a part of this family and I have as much right to speak as anyone else."

Sam wondered what was coming next as his sister-in-law glared at his brother.

"I don't care if you're gay, Sam. It makes no difference to me, and we've known each other long enough for me to know you wouldn't endanger my children, or any other child. I've never said anything to you, Stuart, about the words you've sometimes said — your casual homophobia. Oh, I've heard you at the garage with your mates, and some of the so-called banter has made me cringe. You might say it isn't serious, or you don't mean anything by it, but it's discrimination, plain and simple. What if Andy or Archie turns out to be gay?"

"They won't."

"You can't be so definite, Stuart. They're three and four now, but when they are older, they could be gay, or bisexual, or even transgender — you just don't know. Are you going to throw out your own child, or stop loving them because they don't conform to your expectations, because I'm not. Sam is your brother and deserves better than this from you, from all of you. He's still the same reliable, kind, loving man I've always admired."

By now tears dripped from Sam's cheeks. If he had expected such a passionate defense to come from someone, it would not have been Aisling.

"Aisling is right," Sandie agreed, hugging her two boys. "I would be the same if it was our children. Sam's gay. So what? Darach McNaughton is too, and Tosh Mackintosh. Then there's Davy Kerr and his husband Jason, and Zac and Seth at the hotel, and even the writer and the bloke who was head teacher at the primary school. They're people like anyone else going on with their lives."

"Why is everyone cross, Mummy?" Archie, the eldest asked.

Everyone in the room remained silent for a moment until Jenny's ear-splitting wail cut through the tension.

"It's all right, Archie, sometimes grown-ups can be silly."

"I think it's time everyone shuffled off home." Sam's father rose from his armchair. "You've given us a lot to take in, Sam, but Aisling and Sandie are right. You're our son, and we will always love you and welcome you into our house, but you've given us a shock and we need to think about what we've heard. I don't care if you're gay, and we've no belief in your church. When you announced that you intended to become a minister, it was a shock, but the HIV... That's something else. We'll talk again, but not now."

"All right, Dad."

His mother nodded, and gradually everyone rose, collected their belongings and left the room. Neither of his parents hugged him, but both Aisling and Sandie made a point of doing so outside.

"Don't worry. I'll speak to him," Aisling whispered in his ear.

He mumbled a thanks and stared after them as they left.

"You haven't said much," he said, turning to Gus.

Gus moved quickly toward him, wrapped his arms around Sam's back and kissed his cheek. "I've known about you being gay for ages," he said. "I used to follow you around when I was younger. I've always been good at hiding, and I don't miss much. Darach says that's why I'm a good copper, because I'm skilled at reading people and their body language. Maybe I have gaydar, even if I'm not gay. I work with the kids at the school as well, and we should find time to talk about the youth club. Anyway, as I said, I used to follow you around. You were always nicer to me than the others and didn't tell me to bugger off like them. I overheard the odd phone conversation, listening at doors. When you're the youngest, no one notices you half the time. And I'm more informed regarding HIV because we have training in how to deal with possible scenarios at work."

"I guess I wasn't as good at hiding it as I thought I was."

Gus grinned at him. "No, you weren't."

With Mel already in their car, Gus slipped into the passenger seat and wound down the window. "Oh, and I hope you've told Tosh about your HIV status. He's *the* someone, isn't he?"

"What? How on earth?"

"I told you my observation skills are second to none, and I had a chat with Darach. I hoped you'd tell us eventually."

"You won't say anything to Darach, will you? I know he's your partner, but it's early days with Tosh and me, and he has a lot of baggage, like me, to get over."

"I won't say anything, but Darach can be like a dog with a bone at times, and he's sometimes overly protective of Tosh. Telling us is the beginning, Sam. If you and Tosh are serious, there are an awful lot more people who will find out. People who'll be worse than our Stuart."

"I know what we're up against." With a heavy heart, Sam waited until Gus and Mel drove away then noticed his parents stood at the window. He tried to smile and managed a wave before climbing into his own car and making the short journey back to the manse. Gus was right about one thing.

Today had only been the beginning.

Chapter Eleven

Tosh switched his phone to loudspeaker. "So you told them?"

"I said, didn't I?"

"You told them everything, including your HIV status?"

"Yes, I told them everything. I know it's late for you, but have you listened to a word I've said?"

"I'm sorry, Sam, but I wasn't sure you'd go through with it."

"Well, I did."

"Are you pouting?" Tosh asked, chuckling. "It sounds like you're pouting from here."

"I might be. Tell me what you're wearing?"

Tosh's cock stirred as Sam lowered his voice to a sexy growl. "Oh, no you don't," Tosh said. "I want more details than you just told them."

"Mum and Dad were all right, but me being HIV positive has hit them for six. Gus said he already knew I was gay. Alec was annoyed I hadn't told him everything. Aisling and Sandie were amazing, and Stuart was a dick. Now, tell me what you're wearing."

Tosh rolled onto his back. "I might have guessed Stuart would be the least supportive. What about Hamish?"

"I'll have to call him, I suppose, and you haven't answered my question."

Tosh reached down and idly stroked his now semi-hard cock. "Actually, I'm not wearing anything but a smile."

Sam's breath hitched.

"Care to share your night-time ensemble to me?" Tosh asked.

"I'm not wearing anything either—too hot for clothes."

"You most certainly are. As far as I'm concerned, you're always too hot for clothes, though I do love a man in a suit." Tosh leaned over and grabbed the lube from the bedside cabinet. He placed the phone on his chest then squeezed a blob of the cool liquid onto his fingers and stroked himself once more.

"Are you doing what I think you're doing?" Sam asked.

"What do you think I'm doing?" Tosh teased.

"You know what I think."

"Go on. Say it. Tell me out loud, Sam. I want to hear you."

"Oh, God. The things you do to me, Brodie Mackintosh."

"I hope you're stroking your cock, because I am."

"Yes, Tosh," Sam growled. "I've grabbed the lube, pulled back the sheet, and now I'm stroking myself languorously. I've always loved that word. My cock is hard and leaking. If I close my eyes, I can see your fingers wrapped around your silky flesh. I can hear your breath as it catches. You're arching your back now, aren't you?"

"Shit, Sam, talk dirty to me. If you keep that up, I'm going to come now. I wish I could see you."

"I wish I could see you too. I want to bury my face into your neck, lick those beads of perspiration, and sniff air filled with the smell of sex."

Tosh turned his head, buried his face and bit into his pillow. A few more strokes and he'd be there.

"Someday, Tosh, I want you to fuck me. I want to feel you inside me."

"Yes," Tosh yelled, sending streams of cum over his hand and stomach, milking himself until he was spent. At the other end of the phone, Sam moaned then panted heavily. Tosh stared at his ceiling. Could he do it? Could he fulfill Sam's wish?

"You okay?" he asked, wiping himself with some of the tissues he kept by the bed.

"Yeah, I'm fine." Tosh thought he detected doubt and uncertainty in Sam's voice.

"About what I said, there's no pressure, Tosh. I don't expect you to take any risks."

Tosh thought for a minute. "I want to, Sam, but I have to be certain. I know there's more risk if you fuck me." He yawned, unable to stop himself. Sam had been right. It was late for him.

"You must be tired, Tosh, and you have an early start tomorrow."

"It's been a big day for you too," Tosh replied, his lids threatening to close.

"Very big," Sam replied. "Maybe sometime soon we could do this in the same room."

"I'd like that. Goodnight, Sam. I'll see you soon."

"Night, Tosh."

He reached over and switched off the bedside lamp. Maybe he'd pay Stuart a visit in the morning while on his round. After all, he had knowledge of Stuart that his brothers didn't. Sometimes, being a postman proved useful.

* * * *

"Morning, Stuart. I have your post." Tosh breezed into the garage midmorning, pleased to find Stuart Carmichael alone in his office. "Looks like bills today. Nothing in a plain wrapper for you this time."

Tosh was gratified to see Stuart's head jerk up after his deliberately provocative comment. He wanted to get Stuart on the wrong foot. "Oh, did you think us postmen couldn't work out when our customers have received such discreet packages? We know the names these companies use. I've had deliveries of a similar nature myself."

"So I suppose you've heard what happened, then. The gay grapevine must have been buzzing last night. I suppose Sam told Darach, and he told you, or had you already guessed about my brother, using some sort of gaydar?"

Tosh made a mental note to speak to Darach. "Sam's a good man. You should be proud to have him as a brother."

"You have no idea about my feelings for Sam. Anyway, I'm fed up of getting it in the neck. Aisling gave me what-for last night."

"I've always admired your wife. She's created great websites for people and companies, *and* managed not to kill you. Still, I've always thought she wore the trousers in your house." He grinned, knowing it would get under Stuart's skin.

"Is that all you've got, Tosh?"

"Oh, no. I have more than that. I've often wondered about your choices, whether you've ordered any of the more interesting sets of toys. Maybe handcuffs or a dominatrix costume for Aisling. I can see her dressed in a black corset and stockings with suspenders, paired with thigh-high boots with five-inch heels."

The flush on Stuart's face told Tosh he'd hit a nerve, so he continued. "Maybe you should purchase a strap-on for her and discover what we know about the joys of having your prostate pounded." By now he'd expected Stuart to come out punching, but instead he gulped. Tosh leaned forward as Stuart edged back. He lowered his voice to a whisper.

"Or have you already? That's it, isn't it? Oh, I can see it now, you bent over the bonnet of a car with her hitting your sweet spot with every thrust, grabbing your hair, pulling your head back and making you come over the grill with your jeans pooled around your ankles. Her whispering what a good boy you are while you groan and beg for more. You're nothing but a bloody hypocrite."

"Piss off, Tosh." He wiped his overall-covered arm across his brow but stayed on the other side of his desk.

"Finding it a bit hotter now, Stuart? Don't get up to see me out. I wouldn't want you to have to reveal your hard-on under the table." Tosh straightened. Maybe he'd let his temper take this too far. "Look, I don't want to fight with you, Stu. We've always got on, or so I thought. I know Sam's condition must have come as a shock…" *Damn, why did I say that?* He needed a distraction. Would Stuart notice?

"You didn't keep your dick in your trousers when you were young, either. And I bet you weren't always careful. No one is perfect, and family should stick together. I wish I'd had brothers when I was growing up."

Stuart slumped over the table and held his head up with his hands. "He always seemed so…straight, if that's not ridiculous, *and* he had girlfriends. I suppose *they* weren't real. He's a minister, Hamish is a teacher and Gus is a plod. Me—I've always been the thick one—just a mechanic. Me and Alec didn't go to university like the other three. Alec was expected to carry on with the business, and I wasn't interested. When Sam got into Glasgow, Mum and Dad were so proud, and now this. I can't believe he's just so matter of fact about having HIV. This could kill him."

"No one can live forever," Tosh said quietly.

Stuart stared at him wide-eyed. "Bloody hell, I'm sorry. I didn't think about Harry."

"It's all right, Stuart. People have been walking on eggshells around me for too long. If what happened to Harry has taught me one thing, it's that you have to live for the here and now and get your happiness where you can, because you don't know what life will throw at you. I miss him every day, but Harry wouldn't have wanted me to sit around grieving forever. And let's face it, either of us could get run over by a bus tomorrow. Sam has lived with this virus for over ten years, on his own."

If there was ever a light bulb moment, Tosh was sure he'd just witnessed one when Stuart frowned at him. "You knew, didn't you? You knew about him being gay and HIV positive. Darach didn't ring you this morning and tell you what happened yesterday, did he? It's you, isn't it? You're the someone in his life. All this moving-on crap. You're fucking my brother. Well I never. This is a turn-up for the books."

Tosh wasn't sure what to say. This hadn't gone how he'd planned at all. "Talk to Sam, Stuart. He thinks you're an ignorant dick who's ashamed of him. But the real truth is, you've got a chip on your shoulder and think you're not as clever as your brothers."

Stuart held up his hands. "All right, I admit I *was* a dick yesterday. Aisling showed me a lot of information last night. After, I sat in the boys' bedroom and stared at them while they slept and couldn't imagine not loving them. And Sam would never put them in danger."

"Then tell him that and put him out of his misery." Tosh opened the office door. "I'll bring my car in next week for its MOT."

"You do that. Wednesday works for us — any time."

Stuart's assistant lifted his head and glanced toward them. Tosh nodded and strode out the door. He had no idea how Sam would react to Stuart knowing of their relationship. He needed to speak to him first. After pulling out his phone, he texted Sam to come round to his place for dinner. Sam's reply of *yes* appeared quickly. After the fun of their recent activities, Tosh wondered if Sam would be quite so thrilled to find out what had happened at the garage or about his plans to visit the doctor's surgery.

* * * *

Tosh tapped his foot to the rhythm in his head, so nervous he considered bolting out of the waiting room more than once. Ellis McKenzie had been his doctor for many years and had agreed to squeeze him in as his last appointment of the day. Tosh had questions, and he needed answers. The receptionist called out his name and he made his way through the double doors and down a small corridor. When he pushed the door open, the doctor looked up from behind his desk. He smiled, a more common occurrence since the birth of his daughter. It was well known he and his wife had been trying for years. There were few secrets in such a small population, a fact which made Tosh even more nervous about his and Sam's relationship.

"Tosh, what can I do for you that's so urgent? You said

you wanted to pick my brain."

Tosh gulped and gripped the arms of the chair. "This is confidential, isn't it?"

"Of course it is. You know better than to ask. Anything you tell me stays between us. What's on your mind?"

"No, I'm fine. You know me, walking in all weathers keeps the bugs and viruses away. I wanted to ask you about something, a treatment I've heard of. I don't know if you can get it in the UK yet."

"A treatment for what?" The doctor sat forward in his seat.

"It's called PrEP. It's for people who—"

"I know what PrEP is for, but why would you be interested... Unless you're contemplating sleeping with someone who is HIV positive." The doctor's eyes widened as the penny dropped. "Ah. Right. Okay. Well, what I can tell you is that it won't be available on the National Health Service any time soon. There have been studies which have shown PrEP is almost one hundred percent successful in preventing HIV being passed on, but NHS England has decided not to offer it on prescription. Nothing has been announced for Scotland yet, but there are campaigns ongoing."

"That's daft if it's so good."

"I agree with you. It wasn't a decision made by doctors. I won't bore you with the reasons given. I could prescribe it privately, but I've no idea of the cost. I'd have to investigate, and you'd have to be assessed and take an HIV test yourself. I can do that for you, or you could go to a clinic. Is there any chance your status has changed since you were last tested?"

"No."

"Look, Tosh. I'm not going to lecture you on safe sex, as I'm sure you're not going to take any risks, and the other person has been honest enough to share their status with you. I'm sure he's aware of the risks as well. Have you discussed the situation, you and this person?"

Tosh had the feeling Ellis McKenzie had a good idea of

the identity of the other man. "We've discussed it, but it's early days. I thought if I took this new drug, then, if we had an accident, I might be protected. They have it in the US, don't they? Would you prescribe it?"

"I'll check on the situation for you if you're certain. You'd have to commit to taking it every day, and it doesn't work straight away, but after a couple of weeks you get protection. You realize it's not a substitute for condoms, don't you?"

"I do, but I thought I'd find out what you knew first."

The doctor leaned forward in his chair. "I want to say it's good you're able to consider a future and another relationship but…"

"You just did, Ellis, and it's okay, I don't mind."

"This relationship isn't going to be easy for either of you."

Now Tosh was certain Ellis McKenzie knew exactly who he was talking about. "No, it isn't. I'm not going to mention his name, but as you're likely to be his doctor as well, I'm guessing you know who the other person is. I wouldn't be surprised if he turned up here himself. Will you let me know what you find out?"

"I'll make inquiries, but I can't promise anything. Remember, you should be careful with oral as well as anal sex, and check for any cuts, no matter how small, though I'm sure you're aware of the relative dangers of all sexual practices. And if you are worried, or the condom splits, there's a tablet you take every day for a month that works a bit like a Morning After Pill."

Heat rushed into Tosh's cheeks. Discussing anal sex with his doctor wasn't his favorite pastime, but if he was grown up enough to do it, he should also be prepared to talk about it. He smiled. "You made sure I knew everything there was to know when I told you I was gay all those years ago. I'd have given Rudolph a run for his money, my face was so red after listening while you gave me the safe-sex lecture."

"And there I was trying to be so matter-of-fact about it. We were both so much younger. It was so brave of you coming out back then — you and Darach."

"And now Zac is out as well and settled down. We've practically got a gay mafia up here now, what with Davy and Jason, and even the older gays. Maybe we'll become a gay mecca — now *that* would be funny."

"Be careful, Tosh, but be happy as well. HIV might not be the death sentence it once was but it's reckoned over one hundred thousand people in the UK have it and lots don't even know they do. People can be careless."

"You don't have to tell me, Doc. I suppose that's the one advantage of living up here — less opportunity."

"Maybe you're right, Tosh. I'll let you know when I find anything out and we'll sort out a date for a test to be certain."

Tosh stood to leave. "Thanks, Ellis. People say you're grumpy, but I've never seen that side of you. How's the little one doing?"

"She is crawling everywhere, and away with you before I let my grumpy side loose."

Tosh grinned. "Thanks, Doc. You know I've always appreciated your support."

"Just be happy, Tosh. We all deserve a little happiness in our lives."

Strolling back to his house, Tosh considered everything Ellis had told him. He'd hoped he would be able to protect himself with more certainty, but he would have to wait, for now. He had a lot to contemplate as well as worrying how the hell he was going to explain outing their relationship to Stuart.

Chapter Twelve

"Stuart knows about us."

Sam spluttered, nearly choking on the mouthful of food he'd been chewing. "Stuart knows what? And how does he know? Shit, Tosh, what did you do?" He couldn't believe what he'd heard. "Of all the people."

"I had to go round to his garage this morning to deliver his post, and, well, it sort of came out."

Sam clattered his fork onto the table. "Shit! Go on. Tell me. How the hell does such information *sort of* come out?"

"I may have goaded him."

"For fuck's sake, Tosh, and now I'm swearing. What did you say?"

"I couldn't help myself. I didn't like what he'd said about you. I've never thought he was homophobic. He's always kept his thoughts to himself around me, and I've been delivering his post for years. There's this company online that sells, you know, *adult* products. They use another name on their parcels to be discreet, so I knew he'd had some items delivered."

Now Sam was intrigued. All sorts of possibilities crossed his mind. "All right, so what did you say?"

"I suggested he might like to get Aisling a strap-on and let her pound his prostate for him, so he could enjoy the experience for himself."

Glad not to have food in his mouth, Sam nearly gave in and smiled. Instead, he fashioned a frown. "And?"

Tosh gazed at him with a twinkle in his eye. "And from the expression on his face, I think they may have already enjoyed that particular activity."

Sam pressed his hand to his mouth to smother a laugh, but he couldn't stop the tears falling down his face, or the image in his mind. A loud guffaw burst out from behind his hand and his whole body shook.

"Sam, are you all right?"

"I'm fine," he managed. "Oh, God, I wish I'd been a fly on the wall for your conversation."

"You're not mad at me?"

"Not for that, but how *did* he find out about us?"

"I accidentally mentioned I knew about you being HIV positive for so many years. At first, he thought Darach had told me, because you'd told him, but then he put two and two together. If it's any consolation, I think he's regretting what he said. It sounds like Aisling tore several strips off him last night. Maybe she's locked a cock cage on him as punishment, or perhaps she paddled him on her lap."

"Oh, God, stop. Please. I'm going to have to wash out my mind with bleach at this rate." Sam picked up his glass and swallowed a few mouthfuls of water. "I'm hoping he didn't mean what he said yesterday as well, and was merely shocked and concerned for the boys. Did he say anything about us?"

"I think he was surprised, but he didn't say he'd tell anyone, and Alec knows already."

"Gus is fine. Umm, he guessed about us. Seems he's a pretty good detective, and he works with Darach. And there's Jason, his best friend. I've still got to call Hamish. I feel guilty he's the only one of the family who doesn't know."

"And your mum and dad? How will they feel about me?"

"They've known you for years. It'll be fine, Tosh. My family will keep the information to themselves, but the more people who know, the more likely it'll get out. Maybe I could do a sermon. There are plenty of passages that deal with throwing the first stone, not judging others, forgiveness—"

"And loving your neighbor?" Tosh suggested.

"And that one too. This is real, isn't it? This is really happening." Sam shivered as if someone had walked across his grave. "Are you sure you want this, Tosh? When the shit hits the fan, so to speak, you and your family will get caught in the crossfire."

"Some will say I'm a filthy papist trying to sully your reputation and lead you into sin."

Sam put his hand to his forehead. "I'd never even considered that one, but you're right. Some of them would agree with that view, even though you've attended the church a few times. They might be more upset at me having a lapsed Catholic for a boyfriend than they would us being gay." He pondered Cormac Campbell, one of the elders, and had no doubt he'd say the anti-Christ was attempting to corrupt a follower of the True Faith. He pushed his plate away, his appetite gone, glanced up and witnessed the worried expression on Tosh's face.

"We can stop this now," Tosh said, reaching out his hand to take hold of Sam's fingers. "If it's too much, before either of us gets in too deeply."

Sam considered Tosh's words for a few moments. What he said made sense, but he didn't want to stop. He wanted Tosh in his life and in his bed. If he lost this particular job, there were other places that wouldn't object to a gay minister, and it wasn't as if he'd lose his family over the choice. They weren't religious and they'd accept Tosh into the family fold. And the truth was, he was already in too deep and halfway to falling in love with the man opposite him, who hadn't run away when he'd revealed his status. He threaded his fingers through Tosh's.

"I don't want to stop. Do you?"

"No, but it's not going to be easy for many reasons."

Sam forced back the niggling thought in the rear of his mind — the one that popped up sometimes when he was alone, in the middle of the night. No, he didn't want to go on living this half-life, denying himself things others took for granted simply because they were straight. Strangely, although he'd worried about letting his parents down, he'd never believed he was letting God down. He trusted in his belief, and it had comforted him on many a long, dark night. No, he wasn't afraid of God, only the views of men. Emerging from his thoughts, he realized Tosh had paused. He appeared nervous, so Sam waited for what Tosh would say next, especially when he broke eye contact and gazed at the half-eaten food on his own plate.

"I visited Ellis McKenzie today."

Sam sat up in his seat. "Oh."

"I wanted his advice. I've been checking the Internet, but you know how unreliable information can be on there. I asked him about taking PrEP, but it's not likely to be available on general prescription. They've carried out a study about its effectiveness, and the results so far have been good. He did say he might be able to prescribe it privately, and he'd check out the situation for me."

Sam wasn't sure what to say. His heart leaped into his throat that Tosh was prepared to do this for him, for them. "I couldn't ask you to take medication because of me," he whispered. "What if there are side effects, and how much would it cost? Did you mention me?"

"No, of course I didn't, but I suspect he guessed. You are one of his patients, and I assume he's aware of your status."

"He is. He's been great. I thought he'd give me one of his looks and a lecture, but he didn't. I still don't like the idea of you taking a drug they haven't allowed to be prescribed."

"But if it works and it protects me, we wouldn't have to worry so much — you know. We'd still have to use condoms, but taking it would lessen my chances of infection. Anyway, these days HIV isn't a death sentence, is it? You said as much."

Sam stood, sending his chair over to clatter onto the stone floor. He gripped the table and leaned forward. "Don't you dare be blasé about this disease, HIV can still kill you. Every person is different. I'm one of the lucky ones. I've seen people die slowly and painfully, young people Jock has worked with who sold themselves on the street after their parents threw them out and it was the only way they could survive. They sold their bodies, then their pimps would get them hooked on whatever it took for them to blank out the memories. I'm lucky, the HIV drugs work for me, but it's not the same for everyone and nothing is one hundred percent safe." He stepped back, not knowing what to do or say.

"I'm sorry, Sam. I didn't mean to sound blasé. I've read the stories online too. I thought it might help if you weren't worried about me all the time. There are lots of ways for us to be together. Let's not argue. Go and sit on the sofa. I'll make us a mug of tea and we can cuddle and discuss the youth center."

Sam nodded, grateful to be able to change the subject. He'd make an appointment to see Ellis McKenzie himself. "I'd like that. I've had some ideas and the manager of the community center has agreed to let us use the building a couple of nights a week until we find somewhere else."

Tosh rose from his seat and came around to hug Sam from behind, wrapping his arms around Sam's chest. He leaned back and Tosh sucked on his earlobe. The sensation made his cock stir. It amazed him how one simple action could make him feel so much. He moaned, unable to stop himself, and clutched Tosh's hands tighter.

"See?" Tosh said. "We can do all sorts together that feel good, including drinking tea." Sam let go reluctantly and removed himself to the other room to wait on the sofa. He dug in his pocket for the notebook with the suggestions he'd written for the youth club. This would be something positive for the local area, and something much-needed. He'd already put feelers out at the local secondary school and made a list of people who might be prepared to help if he twisted their arms.

"How long have you had this beard?" Tosh asked.

Sam lay on his back with his head in Tosh's lap while Tosh stroked his face.

"I'm not sure, but for much longer than the fashion for them now. I swear, you can't watch a sports event without one of the players having a weird long beard like they're some backwoodsman. I grew it because I wanted to appear older and thought it gave me more gravitas. Why? Don't you like it?"

"I'm not sure. I suppose I'm used to you having one. It's hard to imagine you without it now." He leaned down and kissed Sam lightly. "And it does tickle."

"Maybe you should try growing one."

"I did once, but I'm like my dad. I'm losing hair, not growing it, and despite mine being dark, I don't get much further than the stubble stage. Would you mind me being as bald as a coot as well as not having a six pack? They say you follow your maternal grandfather and mine had no hair from an early age."

"I wouldn't care." He rolled and lifted Tosh's shirt to place tiny kisses across his stomach. "I like the little extra weight you carry. It gives me a soft cushion to put my head on."

"Says the man with the muscles."

"I eat well, Tosh, and I have a rowing machine at the manse. I need to keep healthy, and you like my body. I saw you watching me when we went kite flying and my shirt rode up." He reached under Tosh's shirt and pinched his nipple without warning, making him jerk.

"Shit! You could warn a bloke first."

"Now where would be the fun in that?"

Tosh shifted himself until he lay below Sam. His now hard cock pressed against Sam's thigh. Sam positioned himself so their erections aligned then moved slowly, creating friction, until he elicited a moan from Tosh, who thrust up to meet him. He pushed up Tosh's shirt and latched onto a nipple, sucking hard then licking to soothe it again. Unable to wait any longer, he asked, "Is this all right?"

Tosh nodded. "Please, I need you, need this."

Sam thrust, establishing a rhythm, then kissed Tosh, who

opened his lips and allowed Sam to push his tongue inside, fucking his mouth.

"If we keep doing this, I'm going to come in my pants," Tosh said between breaths, now using his hands to grip Sam's arse and pull him even closer.

"Sounds like a plan to me."

For a few minutes, he lay there meeting Tosh's thrusts, urging their erections together, letting the sensations wash over him until Tosh stiffened beneath him. He wasn't far away himself. He willed his body to come at the same time, concentrating harder. He examined Tosh's wonderful face, waiting until he held his head back, lifted his chin and opened his mouth to gasp for breath. Only then did Sam let his orgasm wash over him, lifting his torso and throwing his head back as he thrust his hips down and a hot rush of wetness exploded from within him. Unable to hold himself up any longer, he collapsed, breathing heavily into Tosh's neck.

For a while, he remained in the same position until the hot feeling in his pants cooled. He needed to clean himself off. "Tosh, are you okay?"

"Of course I am. If a bit sticky."

"Me too. I should clean up, then I'd better get going. The walk home will do me good."

"I'll have a shower after you've gone."

Sam peeled himself away and tidied himself. Once back downstairs, he found Tosh sitting up on the sofa. "Does it show?" he asked.

"No one will see you in the dark, and it's not as if you've a housekeeper waiting at home for you. I wish you didn't have to go."

Sam sat next to Tosh and took hold of his hand. "I wish I didn't have to go either, but it's safer to go now, and you have to get up early in the morning. I'll slip out the back way and go round just in case." He kissed Tosh.

"Are you sure you're all right to help with the youth center? I'm going to the school tomorrow to talk about it, and we're having a meeting to set up a committee and run a few ideas past people."

"I'll be there," Tosh replied. "There'll be enough people for my appearance not to be noticed, I'm sure."

Sam stood.

"I'll come and lock the door behind you," Tosh said, following him.

Maybe one day he wouldn't have to do this—sneak out of the back door like a thief in the night. Outside, the air was still warm. He ducked around the rear of the houses then strolled along the coast road, listening to the waves lap onto the rocky shoreline. He loved this place and he didn't want to leave, but if it meant he and Tosh had a future together, he'd be willing to move. He didn't want to lose the growing warmth in his chest which appeared whenever he mused on his relationship with Tosh. God obviously chose to move in mysterious ways after all, and who was he to argue with God?

Chapter Thirteen

"Mrs. McPherson, how lovely to see you here, and are those boxes of your famous biscuits and muffins that I see?"

"Aye, Reverend. I thought I'd come along and lend a hand to your meeting and lock up afterward. I am a key holder, after all. I'll get plates out for these and put the boiler on so we can have a nice cup of tea, seeing as it's turned a wee bit chilly. That's the summer over for now, I guess. Still, we did well getting a couple of weeks of sunshine. How many will be here tonight?"

"I'm not entirely sure. I expect we'll be playing it by ear for a while. I'll set the chairs out around a few tables. I'm sure I remember there being a flip chart somewhere around here."

"There's one in the cupboard over there. We've a screen and projector as well if you want to set up your laptop thingy to use rather than the chart. We have film nights here with the cinemas being hard to get to for the old folk. Last week we watched *Random Harvest*. Such a lovely film, don't you think?"

"I don't think I've seen it," Sam admitted.

"Really? Well you've missed a treat. Next one is *Casablanca*. Now you'll no be telling me you haven't seen that one."

"I've had the pleasure of watching it a few times. Such a great last line."

Mrs. McPherson paused for a moment. "Aye, I've often wondered about those two." Then she scurried off to the kitchen area before Sam could say anything. He shook his head and continued shifting the chairs from the stacks.

Ten minutes later, the sound of voices drifted in from

outside. Gus pushed through the swinging door first, followed by a tall, handsome redhead and four teenagers, two boys and two girls.

"So, we're the first, are we?" Gus said.

"You are, other than Mrs. McPherson, who is busy making tea. Do I get an introduction, then?"

"Of course." Gus turned toward the young man with the curly ginger hair and cheerful grin. "This is Cameron McAllister. He's not been at the school long, but he was keen to help. As well as teaching technology and science, he's into outdoor pursuits, especially mountain climbing. How many Munros have you bagged?"

Cameron's embarrassed blush only added to his attractiveness, in Sam's opinion.

"One hundred and seventy-three, not that I'm counting or anything. Well, of course I am, or I wouldn't know, but I've more than a hundred to go. I managed to bag a few this summer in the Cullins on Skye. The weather has been kinder this year." He put out his hand.

"I haven't done any climbing I'm afraid, but I like a good walk." Sam shook his hand, feeling the callouses, no doubt from holding onto a rope. "It's good of you to help out."

"A few others on the staff said they'd help as well but couldn't come tonight. I'll introduce you to this lot. These are our head boy, Jack, and head girl, Marie, and deputies, Michael and Ally."

Sam shook their hands. "I hope you didn't get your arms twisted to be here. We want your input because, after all, this place is for you." He thought Michael may have been dragged there, judging from the bored expression on his face, but others showed genuine interest.

The dark-haired girl stepped forward first. "I'm also the chair of the school's rainbow group. I wanted to make sure the youth club would be LGBTQ friendly, you know, with it being run by the church."

Sam noted the grin on his brother's face. "I can assure you, Ally, everyone will be welcome here regardless of, well, anything. The Church of Scotland is not homophobic. This year a resolution passed allowing gay ministers to be married. And I'm sure you are already well aware we've had women ministers since the 1960s."

"Will we be able to show gay films?" she persisted. "My granny comes here for the old folks' films and I thought it would be a chance for us to watch a bigger variety."

"Well, yes, as long as they are suitable and age appropriate."

Jack shrugged and gave Sam a look he recognized. "Come on, Ally, give the poor bloke a rest. Most of us want somewhere to hang out, maybe play pool and darts or watch the football and keep warm. I'm sorry, Reverend. My sister can be pushy."

Sam smiled. "Don't worry, Gus and I have three more brothers. Why don't we sit? Maybe one of you could bring in the projector and screen? Gus, could you help? Mrs. McPherson knows where everything is."

The door flew open again and Sam glanced up to see Brice Drummond wheeling himself through, followed by Darach McNaughton and Tosh. Sam introduced everyone.

"Jason Kerr said he'd come along and maybe give carpentry and general handyman tips if anyone was interested," Brice said.

"That would be great. I'd like to give the kids something other than a place to hang around in."

Tosh had taken the seat on the other side of Cameron. Every now and again, he glanced his way. When everyone had seated themselves, Sam asked for suggestions of possible activities and listed them on the laptop connected to the screen. In a short while, they had a good list of activities, including Brice's offer of art lessons, and the possibility of a reading or writing group led by the local crime writer Richie MacNeill. Mrs. McPherson suggested cake-making. Although he'd never watched the show, The Great British Bake Off was obviously popular among teenagers too.

"And our dad could give us an old banger to do up. Some

good ones come into the scrap yard," Michael added, finally showing some interest in being there.

"My brother could help with that, Jack," Sam said, imagining Stuart's face if he suggested it. "He's a mechanic, or maybe Duncan, his apprentice."

"I'm not good at anything," Tosh said while others offered particular skills. "But I'm happy to help out and maybe organize film nights, or watching a box set. Do any of us know anyone who can play instruments? Maybe in good weather we could persuade Zac McKenzie or Chris Quinton to provide football training, if we get the right premises."

Sam put his hands up to interrupt the talking. "Let's get up and running first, shall we, but those are great ideas."

Over mugs of tea and also biscuits and cake, they discussed dates, times and numbers. The students said they'd do a few surveys around school as well and talk to the PTA about more volunteers, though they weren't keen on having parents around. Sam hadn't been able to talk to Tosh all night, not on his own, anyway. In fact, Tosh had spent much of the evening chatting to Cameron. Something told him the teacher might have a lot more in common with them both than an interest in helping at the club. He pushed away the green-eyed monster lurking just below the surface and, as he gazed around the group talking over their food and drink, he realized perhaps there was an over-representation of gay adults. He feared some parents would worry, especially if he allowed gay-themed films to be shown.

"Can I give you a lift, Tosh?" Cameron's voice cut through the general chatter as they packed away.

Sam resisted the urge to stare.

"Gus is taking the students home, so I've space."

Tosh hesitated and swiftly glanced his way before answering. They'd made no plans to get together after the meeting.

"Um, I came with Darach and Brice."

Mrs. McPherson jangled her keys. "Hurry up and make up your mind, laddie. I've got to lock up and I don't like being out in the dark."

"I'll take you home, Mrs. McPherson," Sam said. "And help put everything away. There's not much to do."

Sam caught Darach's glance in his direction before he spoke. "No, you go with Cameron if you want, Tosh. It'll save Brice and me from going out of our way. And he's bugging me about having to get home to empty the kiln."

Darach stared directly at Sam after he'd spoken, and he knew the man had deliberately encouraged Tosh. He obviously didn't approve of their friendship. If Tosh refused, it would look odd now.

"All right, then. That's kind of you, Cameron."

Tosh glanced over his shoulder as he followed the teacher out of the room. Sam tried to smile, but knew it hadn't reached his eyes.

When Cameron touched Tosh's arm, Sam wanted to dash across the room and drag him off. Instead, he continued stacking the chairs.

"Maybe we could stop for a drink on the way home as well, if you're not in a hurry, Tosh."

Sam stopped what he was doing, waiting for Tosh's reply.

"I think that's everything, Reverend." Mrs. McPherson talked over any chance he had of hearing Tosh.

"Yes, thank you for this evening."

"It's nae bother, and I like being out with the young folk. It makes a change from hearing the old biddies worrying over their blood pressure and cholesterol all the time."

Thinking about his regular visit to the local care homes he had planned for the morning, Sam couldn't help but nod in agreement. "I imagine it would," he said.

* * * *

All night images of Tosh leaning toward Cameron, talking and laughing, filled Sam's head. Cameron was undoubtedly good-looking, and younger, and he didn't have the specters of death and religion hanging over him. If the teacher fancied Tosh, he'd be much better for him than a man in the closet with a dangerous virus flowing through his veins. He stared at the clock next to his bed — two a.m. What if they'd gone home together and Tosh had invited Cameron in for a coffee, and one thing had led to another? Or maybe Cameron had leaned in for a kiss goodnight and left Tosh wondering if he'd made the right choice — if there was a better choice available. If Cameron was a better choice than Sam. Tosh had a right to be happy and safe, to have sex without worrying that he could be infected with a life-threatening illness, didn't he? A maelstrom of thoughts whirled around Sam's mind, tormenting him until exhausted, he finally lapsed into sleep.

* * * *

Sam checked his phone the next morning — nothing. He wrote a text then deleted it in fear it would appear he was checking up on Tosh. Today, he had parochial visits for members of his congregation who could no longer get to church for themselves. He liked visiting the old folk in their own homes but, although they tried hard, he found it harder to visit the local care homes, especially those with many dementia sufferers. Even more, he hated arriving to find one of his regulars had died in the night.

When he'd finished his rounds, he headed out for a stroll along the coastal road from his house, down to the Lodge and onto the path frequented by dog walkers. The day was cool, made worse by the biting wind coming off the sea from the north, but at least it was dry. He wrapped his coat around him, sat on the bench and stared out to sea.

"Penny for them."

Hell, his was the last voice Sam wanted to hear today. He turned to find Darach McNaughton standing behind him.

"Is it all right if I sit?"

"It's a free world, Sergeant."

"I'm on my way home. I've been on early shift this morning. I saw you here and thought I'd come over."

"Very public-spirited of you, I'm sure." Sam gazed out at the birds winging their way across the sky and skimming the gray water.

"Tosh was on good form last night. It's wonderful to see him out and getting involved with something, and Gus says Cameron is a nice bloke."

"Really? Well, we need all the help we can get at the club." Sam dug his hands into his pockets.

"He appeared taken with Tosh. Gus told me he's from Portmahomack. I don't suppose he had much chance to meet men there."

Sam turned to face his old friend. "Shall we cut to the chase, Darach, and stop this shilly-shallying? I assume you know Tosh and I have been seeing each other."

"I do now."

Sam dug his nails into his palm. He wanted to punch something, but perhaps one of the local police wasn't the best choice.

"Tosh told me to mind my own business when I asked him. He said you and he were friends."

Had Tosh talked to Darach earlier? Did Darach know something? Was this a tease before he revealed more? "I suppose you had great fun telling him about us. How I used to get down on my knees for you."

"No, I didn't fill him in on our past. When I talked to him a while back, he wasn't sure about you. I did suggest you might not be exactly straight."

So maybe Tosh hadn't talked to him this morning. "I think he's fully aware of that now."

"What do you want from him, Sam? He's my friend and I love him. I told you before I didn't want to see him hurt again."

"Brodie is a grown man." Sam deliberately chose to use Tosh's proper name again, giving him ownership of it. "He

111

can make his own decisions."

"Yes, he can, but I'm worried with Harry's death, he's not thinking clearly. Getting involved with a closeted minister of the church might not be best for him. You can see that, can't you? Are you prepared to come out to your family and to the church for his sake?"

"So Gus didn't tell you?"

"Tell me what?"

"I told my family. I told them I'm gay. So I *am* out of the closet, at least with them."

"Wow, I never thought I'd see the day. I'm happy for you. Gus didn't say anything, but he's a fine cop and can keep information to himself."

"You're right, he's always been a skilled detective. He already knew about us, or at least suspected. Apparently he used to follow me around in school, but he didn't say anything to anybody. He's a good man, my little brother. You're lucky to have him working with you."

"I am," Darach confirmed. "So is it the job stopping you and Tosh getting together in the open? It might be all right. The police have moved on, so perhaps the church could too."

"It has, but not everywhere, or everyone, feels the same. If I tell people I'm not simply gay but in a relationship, I could get voted out by the kirk session, and I don't want to leave here, Darach."

"Even for Tosh?"

"I doubt he'd want to leave either, and I don't want to have to ask him." Sam was tempted to tell Darach the whole story regarding his HIV status and his past, but he couldn't quite get the words out. Instead, he decided to ask Darach a question. "You know when you found out about Brice's past, did you worry about sleeping with him?"

Darach snorted then coughed. "There were so many reasons why I should have stayed away from Brice."

"But you didn't, even though you knew what that bloke had done to him, how he'd sold himself on the streets and had taken drugs. I'm not judging. I used to work at the Rainbow Tenement in Glasgow. I met lots of young men who—"

"I know that place. It's run by Jock and Joyce Blair. They do excellent work."

"They do. Jock helped me come to terms with being gay, and he inspired me to get involved with the church."

"Small world. Brice told me right from the start what he'd done in the past in an attempt to push me away. I'm not saying it's always been easy for us."

"But he was okay? He'd managed to keep clear of... anything?"

Sam could almost see the cogs shifting into position in Darach's mind.

"Yes, through a combination of luck and protection. Are you trying to tell me something, Sam?"

Was he? Did he want Darach to know? They'd never had the easiest of relationships, and this knowledge might make Darach more certain Tosh should stay well away from him. Would that be better for Tosh? He swallowed hard, letting the words out.

"I'm HIV positive, and yes, Tosh knows. He says it doesn't matter, but I don't know, Darach. I don't want to put him at risk, and I don't want to lose him either."

"Shit! Sam. How long have you known?"

"Since university. But I'm all right. I take my tablets, and I'm as good as I can be. I take care of myself, eat right and get lots of exercise. Last week, I told my family I was gay and that I have HIV. But telling my congregation... I don't know. They might be prepared to accept I'm homosexual, but not my status as well."

"They wouldn't have to know about the HIV, would they? No one needs to know. Bloody hell, Sam. Why didn't you tell me? I could have helped."

Sam shrugged. "You and I haven't ever had that sort of friendship, Darach. So you see, Tosh would be better off with Cameron. He's young, handsome, and he doesn't have this illness hanging over his head. They could fuck each other stupid without worrying."

"Relationships are more than simply sex, you know. There are moves Brice and I can't do because of his disability. It makes us more creative. There are new drugs Tosh could take."

Sam had expected anger, not concern. It confused him and surprised him. "I want him to be happy, Darach, and I want him to be safe. Maybe I was a rebound after Harry. If you want to encourage him to take up with this Cameron, I'll understand. He deserves better than me." Sam realized how pathetic he must sound.

"Tosh can make up his own mind. You're right, I was going to put in my four penn'orth, but if you make him happy, then who am I to interfere? After all, I'm no saint. I left while he stayed here." He glanced at his watch. "I'd better get off. I promised Brice some of my sister's best bread to make bacon sandwiches, and I'm running late, not that he'd notice if he's in the middle of something. He's a pain for not eating regularly."

"I'm glad you're happy, Darach. I hope I'll get an invitation to the wedding."

Darach rose from the bench. "Why don't I drop you home?"

"Thanks, it is chilly now."

"And yes, of course I'll invite you. Brice fancies a Christmas wedding."

Sam dug his hands into his pockets once more and strolled alongside Darach back to his car. He had so much to mull over, and he still hadn't heard from Tosh.

Chapter Fourteen

By late afternoon, Sam couldn't wait any longer. He picked up his phone and called Tosh, but it diverted straight to voicemail. What if Tosh had fallen off his bike on his round and been knocked into a ditch, or what if he'd tripped on the stairs, or what if he'd been delivering in the van and had an accident?

When he parked outside Tosh's house, the first thing Sam noticed was the absence of Tosh's Fiat. Where the hell was he? He shifted his car into gear and drove across the small town to the new estate where Tosh's parents had a bungalow, and breathed a sigh of relief when he saw Tosh's car parked outside. Seeing one of his parishioners, dog lead in hand, Sam wound down a window.

"Hello, Reverend Carmichael. Heard what happened, then. But the Mackintoshes are Catholic, aren't they, not one of our lot."

Sam tried to keep his voice on an even keel. "My sat nav must have brought me down the wrong road. These estates fool it every time. What's happened, then?"

"From what the next door neighbor told me, you know, Mrs. Milner, works in the women's clothes shop in the high street, nice woman, but does like to gossip."

Sam tapped the wheel. "About the Mackintoshes?"

"Oh yes, I'm sorry. I've a habit of going off on a tangent. It drives the wife mad and now I'm doing it again. Seems Mr. Mackintosh had a heart attack last night. There were flashing lights and sirens keeping people awake. Took him off to Elgin, they did."

Sam didn't know what to do. Most of him wanted to

drive straight to the hospital, but the Mackintoshes *were* Catholics, and it would look odd if he turned up. "Is Mr. Mackintosh okay?"

"I don't exactly know. They'd have called old Father McGuire, no doubt, if he needed Last Rites. Bad business all round. I'd best be off. I'll see you on Sunday, Reverend."

Sam nodded, his thoughts elsewhere. Surely, if Tosh's father had died, he and his mother would have returned by now, so maybe they were still at the hospital. It would explain why Tosh hadn't answered his phone. All he could do was wait. He couldn't even go and comfort Tosh as a friend.

A taxi pulled up in front of the bungalow just as he put his car into gear. Tosh emerged from the cab, tired and pale. He saw Sam immediately and trudged toward him.

"You heard about Dad, then? Why don't you come in? Mum's sent me home to get a couple of hours sleep and to collect toiletries for him."

Sam climbed out of the car and, without explanation, left the older man standing there and followed Tosh into the house. Once the door was closed and they were out of sight, Tosh leaned into him. Sam wrapped his arms around Tosh's back and held him tightly, letting him cry on his shoulder.

"He could have died, Sam. It's lucky Mum was a nurse and knew what to do, and the paramedics got here quickly. Apparently, he'd been complaining of indigestion for a while, but you know how it is. They've fitted a stent, and they're going to transfer him to Aberdeen for a triple bypass. He was so close to dying, Sam. I can't lose someone else I love, not so soon after Harry."

"I'll make us a pot of tea. You go and sit on the sofa. Have you had anything to eat?"

"No, not really. You won't know where anything is."

"I'm sure I'll manage to find the fridge. Now, do what I tell you."

Sam rustled up a round of sandwiches and tea, found a tray and carried them through to the living room. Tosh lay on the sofa fast asleep, so Sam sat in the armchair and watched him, chewing slowly, contemplating the thought of losing Tosh. This was not the time to discuss Cameron, but there probably wasn't anything to find out anyway. He picked up a puzzle book and glanced at the crosswords while Tosh snored quietly and steadily. His own eyelids became heavier by the second and appeared determined to close as he stretched and yawned.

* * * *

Sam jumped at the sound of his name. "Sam, Sam, wake up. We both fell asleep." He glanced at the clock. Two hours had somehow passed. Tosh's phone buzzed. He picked it up and stared at the screen.

"I need to get back to the hospital."

"You haven't eaten anything," Sam said. "Here, take this up with you and I'll heat us soup and put it in a flask. I saw one in the cupboard."

"Thanks. That would be a great help."

Sam waited until Tosh was out of the room then reached over to the phone. He knew he shouldn't be doing this, but he couldn't help himself. He checked the last message.

Thxs 4 last nght. Do it again sometime? Cam.

He dropped the phone as if it were on fire then placed it back, telling himself it could mean anything. Soup. He needed to concentrate on helping Tosh and not ask any questions about Cameron, or what had happened last night. He had no right—they weren't a couple, not really. They'd had a few—what to call them?—intimate encounters, but that was all. Tosh owed him nothing.

"You all right?" Tosh asked, finding him stirring in the kitchen. "You were staring into space."

"Yes, I'm fine. I spoke to Darach this morning. He practically interrogated me and said Gus had mentioned Cameron."

Tosh stared back at him, eyes wide. "I don't believe this. My father is in hospital and you're wondering about me and Cameron."

"No," Sam protested. "I was worried when you didn't text me or call all day. That's why I came here tonight to see if you were here when your car wasn't at your house. I thought you might be in a ditch or something, come off your bike."

"I can't deal with this now. I have to go."

Sam poured the soup into the flask and placed it into a bag with the rolls he'd buttered and wrapped.

"Here, take these and eat something. I'm sorry I—"

"I haven't time now. It's dark and I have to get to Elgin. Dad's not out of the woods until he has this operation. I don't know when I'll be able to see you again."

"Oh, all right. I understand."

Tosh grabbed the bag and hurried to the front door. He held it open and Sam stepped through and down the path to his car. "Call me when you know anything," he said.

Tosh was already halfway into his car. He glanced over at Sam then drove off into the night.

What the fuck? Had Sam come to see if he was okay, or to check on his whereabouts and what had happened the night before? Yes, he'd had a drink with Cameron because the man wanted company and someone to talk to. He was a long way from home, and just discovering there were other gay men in the vicinity. They'd discussed football and their jobs, and had told each other funny stories over a pint. On the doorstep, Cameron had asked if he could see Tosh again. All right, maybe the temptation had been there—the chance to have a relationship uncomplicated by the issues surrounding him and Sam—but he'd explained there was someone in his life, and Cameron had accepted it without question and said he needed friends. And now this. Tosh wanted to be angry, but he didn't have the energy.

He found his mother sitting in the armchair next to his

father's bed, clutching her rosary beads, offering up prayers.

"Mum, I'm back." She leaned into his arm when he touched her shoulder. Somehow in the last twenty-four hours she'd aged ten years, her gray hair now more prominent than it had been before.

"They're going to transfer him to the new hospital in Aberdeen tonight and operate tomorrow. Can you drive me there? I have to be with him."

"Of course, Mum. I brought you clothes and a few bits. I made soup. It'll keep warm in the flask. You can drink it in the car, and get some sleep as well."

Nurses appeared and wheeled his father out of the room.

"We'd better get going, Mum. I saw the new hospital on the news, so I've a good idea where we're going." He threaded his arm through his mother's and they hurried back to the car park. She managed a little soup before falling asleep, leaving him alone, driving in the dark along the A96.

He loved his parents and they loved him, despite everything that had happened in the past. They had tried for years before his mother had finally managed to keep a child full term. The doctors told her Tosh was it, and they'd spoiled him rotten. He'd been fifteen when he'd watched *Queer as Folk* and had truly understood where his sexual interest lay, but hadn't said anything to his parents, or his best friend. Then Darach had touched him and everything had changed. Eventually, after he'd come out, Father McGuire had given up berating his parents. It appeared love truly did conquer all, but unsurprisingly, Tosh had stopped going to Mass. By the time he'd met Harry, his mum and dad had no qualms about their son getting married, even if it wasn't in church, and to a man. And now his father was in an ambulance somewhere on the road ahead. Yes, it was hypocritical, but Tosh offered up a prayer anyway.

Arriving in Aberdeen, Tosh took out his phone and checked for local hotels. He rang ahead and booked two adjoining rooms. His mother would no doubt want to go straight to the hospital, but they were keeping his father sedated until after the operation. She woke just as he drove into the floodlit car park.

"We need to get some sleep, Mum, or we'll be no good to Dad when he wakes after the operation."

"But…"

"No buts, Mum. Come on."

After they'd registered and had been taken up to the third floor, he left his mother in her room and entered his own via the connecting door. Too tired to do much thinking, he undressed and used the bathroom. After settling in bed, he turned on his phone. Sam had messaged him.

I'm sorry. Give me another chance to show you how much you mean to me.

Typical Sam, writing in whole words.

In Aberdeen with mum. Operation tomorrow. Will call when I can. A few prayers might help.

Perhaps he should have given Sam more. Tosh wished Sam was there with his arms wrapped around him, keeping him safe, his beard tickling Tosh's shoulder and neck as he cuddled in behind him. He lay on the bed, staring at the ceiling, letting his mind wander. The image it provided was a vision of Sam, smiling on the beach, pulling at a kite, before he drifted into sleep.

Chapter Fifteen

Despite his exhaustion from the previous day, Sam had risen at seven on Saturday and was currently sipping from a huge mug of tea, having consumed three rounds of heavily buttered toast his arteries would not thank him for. His laptop lay open on the table, its blank page sneering at him. He'd meant to write his sermon the day before, but events had conspired against him.

Early Friday morning, Gus had called and he'd ended up speaking to the older students at the school about the youth club and the activities they were planning. He hoped it wouldn't be too successful or they wouldn't manage to get everyone in the space. After the talks, he'd found himself in the staffroom with Cameron on a non-contact lesson, annoyed at his brother for leaving him. Had he done it deliberately? Was his little brother trying to match-make? Sam couldn't help thinking there was a certain irony in that.

"You must know lots of people around here," Cameron had said, taking a seat after handing Sam a coffee.

"I suppose so. I was brought up in the next village, and I've been minister here for several years. Having four brothers also helps."

"Gus is great with the kids. He's the youngest, isn't he? So where do you come on the list?"

"Right in the middle. Alec is the oldest, then Stuart. They're both married and live locally. Then there's Hamish after me. He's a teacher as well, lives in Stirling. What about you?" He nearly said Tosh had told him he wasn't from around here, but stopped himself in time.

"I come from a small village up north along the A9. My

parents ran a hotel and restaurant."

"Do you see them much?" Sam had sensed a story behind Cameron's words.

"No, they didn't take my coming out well. I still talk to my sister, though, and she fills me in on everything."

"That must be difficult."

"It is. Coming here was a big decision, but I like the school and the area. Meeting new people is always difficult, though, and it's hard to tell how someone will react when they find out I'm gay. I was determined from the start of my career not to make a secret of it." He paused, and Sam wondered what was coming next. "I did wonder if, with you being a minister, you'd not want any gay helpers at the youth club, but talking to Tosh, I've discovered there are a few of us around. You know Tosh, don't you?"

"Everyone knows Tosh. He delivers the mail around here. He's had to go off to Aberdeen. His father had a heart attack and is due to have surgery this morning."

Tosh's message when it had arrived later that day had been brief.

Dad's op successful. We need to talk soon.

"Oh, no. Poor Tosh. Do you think he'd mind me calling him later? I mean, I don't know him well, but we had a good chat over a pint."

Sam had swallowed the last of his coffee and stood, preparing to leave. "You might not get an answer if he's still at the hospital. I'd better get off. I'm sure you have marking to do or something, and I've a sermon to write. Will I see you next week?"

"Yes, I'll be there, and thanks again for this morning. I hope we can get to know each other better as well."

Sam had shaken Cameron's outstretched hand and dismissed the thought that maybe Cameron could tell he was gay. He didn't believe in such rubbish.

"Yes, that would be good. I'll see myself out."

He'd kept himself busy for the rest of the day. Firstly, his Parochial duties took him up to the local hospital to visit patients and take communion with those who wanted it. Stepping outside, he'd shaded his eyes against the glow of the sun and decided he needed some air. He'd picked up a sandwich and drink at the supermarket and driven down the coast to stare at the seals. While there, his mother had rung, asking him to come for dinner. He'd given them some time to absorb his declaration, so he guessed it was time to talk. There had been tears and more hugs, and he'd had to give them a detailed breakdown of his condition and its effects, but in the end, they'd said nothing had changed. He was grateful for their love and support. Contemplating what Cameron had said about his parents and the young people Jock and Joyce helped, he knew he was fortunate.

After everything that had happened, he'd collapsed into his bed early, his sermon still unfinished. He'd heard no more from Tosh.

He cleared away the breakfast things and returned to his computer. Instead of typing, he stared out of the window at the clear blue sky. The roses needed dead-heading and the grass could do with a cut. Perhaps when he'd finished his sermon. He turned back to the empty screen. Fifteen minutes later, he'd still written just the heading when the doorbell rang.

Even with the sun shining through the stained glass window in the door, showing the motes of dust sinking to the floor, the hall, with its old-fashioned dark-wood paneling, remained gloomy. A shadow filled the glass. Perhaps it was the postman. The thought immediately reminded him of Tosh and he wondered how he was doing. He opened the door to find himself embraced in a full-on body hug.

"Hamish. What the hell are you doing here?"

"Stuart told me. Do I get to come in?"

Sam moved away from the entrance. "Of course. Come through to the main room. When did you set off?"

"I made good time. There wasn't much on the A9 at five

this morning. I need the loo, and I could kill for a cup of tea." He stopped. "You should have told me, Sam."

"I know, but…"

"Yeah, yeah, but I'm here now and I want to know everything."

He and Hamish had always been close growing up, but in a different way from him and Alec. "It's good to see you, Hammy."

His brother frowned. "Really? We're doing that, Sammy? Must go to the loo."

Hamish ran past Sam, taking the stairs two at a time, leaving Sam to cross the hallway back into the kitchen to put the kettle on for yet another mug of tea.

After a few minutes, Hamish joined him at the kitchen table.

"How the hell have you kept this to yourself for so many years? We would have helped, Sammy. You must have been so lonely, especially when you first found out."

"I've been lucky, I suppose, with how it's affected me. How could I tell them not only was I gay but also infected with something that might kill me?"

"You could say the same about cancer, or lots of other conditions," Hamish protested.

Sam stared down at his steaming mug. The warmth from the tea when he touched it made him shiver, or maybe it was the terrible memory of the day in the doctor's surgery when he'd been told. "It's not the same, Hammy. I made this happen. My stupidity gave me this. I had sex with men, and one of them gave me this. Don't you get it? I could have passed it on myself. I could have brought about someone's death because I was a selfish bastard who fucked around. Do you have any understanding of what it's like to have to live with those thoughts?"

"So you didn't tell us because you were ashamed?"

"Wouldn't you be?"

"And becoming a minister was contrition, payback, for what you'd done. Did you think it would save your soul or something, because that's totally screwed up?"

"No!" He wanted to scream and shout now. He needed to get himself back on an even keel before his anger bubbled over and he did something he'd regret, whatever that might mean. He placed his palms on his knees and took a few deep breaths.

"No, becoming a minister had nothing to do with my status, well, not directly. I always had a form of belief. I suppose I spent too much time with Granny. I haven't told her about anything, by the way. She taught me God was good, kind, forgiving, and that he understands people's weaknesses. I know you'll think it stupid but I prayed, Hammy. I prayed so hard and I got an answer, and I'm glad I did. The church gave me a focus, and despite my condition, it let me in and gave me shelter. I saw the good it does and the need for belief in people's lives. I've always supposed teaching was the same. You do it because you believe in its importance. It's more than a job you do for the money, isn't it?"

"You're right, and I get it. I don't have faith like you do. Sometimes I'd like to, but it's not in me. And teaching is more than what I do for a living. Some days I hate it and want to leave, but somehow something always happens to remind me why I do it."

"I *was* ashamed, Hammy. I still *am* ashamed of what I did and how I behaved, but I was young and naïve, and I paid for it. Now I have to decide how far I want to go with the truth."

"Are you going to come out to the church and your congregation? That's a massive step. Could you lose your job?"

"Maybe. There's something else I have to tell you as well."

"More? Okay, lay it on me, bro."

Sam couldn't help but smile. He'd missed this so much, talking to his brother as they had when they were children. "Alec, Stuart and Gus know but not Mum and Dad. I've been seeing someone. I think it might have gone pear-shaped, but I'm going to do my best to get him back, if he'll have me."

"Am I allowed to know who?"

"Tosh Mackintosh."

"Isn't he the one whose husband was murdered a year ago?"

"Yes. We started out as friends, then it moved on—and, before you ask, he knows everything—but he has his own problems at the moment. His father had a heart attack, and I did something stupid. I got jealous, and now I'm wondering if I shouldn't let him go to find someone else without my baggage."

"Shit! You don't do things by halves, do you? Maybe you need to give each other space. He's been through a lot, and so have you. You've a streak of the martyr running through you."

Sam jerked his head and glared at his brother.

"Oh, Sammy, don't stare at me like that. Come on, you get ill and hide it because you're ashamed of who you are and what you've done. You can tell yourself you've been punished, and you seek to bring peace to others, and don't allow yourself to have your own life, to have someone to love who loves you. How much more of a martyr can you be? And please don't tell me you've been flagellating yourself any other way. That would be too much for me to deal with."

"No, no whips and chains, and no cilice fastened around my leg."

"What the hell is a cilice?" Hamish asked, dipping a biscuit into his tea.

"One of those chain things with spikes you put around your leg. It digs in and gives you pain."

"Oh, like in *The Da Vinci Code*. Nasty. Nah, too much pain for me."

Sam let the comment slide. "Enough of this. What are we going to do while you're here? We'll have to see the family, of course."

"Not this time, Sammy. I'm here for you. Let's have lunch then go watch a game. We haven't been to the footie for ages. I fancy a trip to Inverness to see if we can get tickets for Cally Thistle. If not, we can have a walk round the river, or go dolphin spotting, and tonight we can watch a few films and get blotto."

"I have a sermon to write," Sam protested.

"Well, I'll drive and you can write on the way there and back. I'm not going to take no for an answer."

"All right, and you have a point. It has been a while."

* * * *

"Now, aren't you glad I persuaded you to go?" Hamish said as he drove them home.

"Yes, I'll admit you were right. Chris Quinton was awesome in goal for Cally Thistle. I don't know how he made those saves. You wouldn't guess he's in his mid-thirties. He lives around here as well, and his wife is the chef at the Lodge."

"That's the place on the coast road, isn't it? Where Jed Harris was married. I remember seeing the pictures and reading about them both coming out. At least you wouldn't be national news."

"No, I suppose not." Sam wasn't sure such knowledge helped a great deal. He wrote *amen* on the screen. "Done," he said.

"So what's tomorrow's theme, then?" Hamish asked.

"Perseverance. I mean, take Cally Thistle for example. Who would have imagined them and Ross County being in the Premier League, and there's Rangers having to make their way back?"

"Nothing like a good football analogy."

Later that evening, having ordered Chinese, Sam sat with Hamish in the imposing living room with its high ceilings and big windows overlooking the garden.

"Don't you get fed up with the dark wood in this place?"

Hamish asked. "And some of this furniture must come from the nineteenth century. Can't you change things?"

"Can't say it's ever bothered me, to be honest. As long as it does what it's supposed to do, why worry?"

"And you say you're gay."

"You do realize not all gay men are the same, don't you?"

"Oh, yes."

Something in Hamish's reply set off Sam's curiosity, but the doorbell interrupted his thought.

"Oh good, food." Hamish dug into his backpack. "I brought something to wash it down with too."

"Whiskey and Chinese — seriously?" Sam rose from the sofa and collected the take-away. By the time he'd returned, Hamish had poured them both a dram of whiskey.

"I'm going to need water," Sam said, putting the food on the coffee table.

"Lightweight. Hurry up with the plates and cutlery, and we can start watching something. I brought films too."

When Sam returned to the living room, a selection of DVDs lay on the table. "I see you've gone for a superhero theme, then — *The Avengers*, *X-Men* and *Guardians of the Galaxy*."

"Well, who doesn't love a kick-ass raccoon and a tree that says 'Groot', not to mention a leading man who is easy on the eye?"

There was that niggle in Sam's mind again. "Hammy, is there something you want to tell me? I'm getting this weird feeling you're dropping hints."

His brother knocked back the glass of whiskey in one then poured and swallowed another.

"What is it? Zara's not pregnant, is she?"

"No, of course she isn't. Anyway, we're not serious. We have fun, and we agreed to see other people."

"How modern of you."

A frown crossed his brother's face. "I don't think you have any right to judge my sex life. Do you?"

The conversation was going downhill fast. "No, I don't.

I'm surprised. I thought you two were serious about each other."

"I'm not like Gus, or Alec and Stuart, practically marrying the first girls they go out with. Like you, I played the field at university, and I'm near enough to Edinburgh to have fun where people don't know me. Anonymity helps." He picked up the DVD. "So *Guardians of the Galaxy*, then?"

"Yes, fine." Sam opened the food, getting the feeling Hamish wanted to change the conversation, and spooned rice and chicken in black bean sauce onto his plate. Hamish loaded the film and piled bits of everything on his plate then settled back while the adverts played.

Sam managed a few mouthfuls while Hamish fidgeted with his food rather than eating it.

"Hammy, what's up? I've told you everything. I keep getting the feeling there's more."

Hamish put down his plate and turned to face Sam. He sighed. "I've slept with men. All right, there it is, I've said it. I've slept with men and women, and even both at the same time. You're not the only one with secrets."

Sam coughed and reached for his drink. "Food gone down the wrong way," he spluttered.

Hamish patted him hard on the back.

"It's okay, you can stop." Sam coughed once more then took several more mouthfuls before facing his brother again.

"Why didn't you say anything?"

"Why the hell would I?" Hamish asked. "I've never found anyone I've wanted to settle down with, male or female, so there wasn't any point. I like sex and I have fun, and I'm not bothered about the person's plumbing. There was one person, another teacher, but it didn't work out."

"Male or female?"

"It shouldn't matter, and it doesn't now. So now you know everything, let's eat up and watch this film."

"I'm sorry, Hammy."

"About what?"

"The one who got away. I know how it hurts to love someone and face losing them."

"You haven't lost him yet," Hamish said. "Maybe it's time you stop being a martyr and fight for what you want. You deserve love and happiness as well."

Throughout the film, Sam tried to process what Hamish had said. So many secrets. Did anyone truly know anyone else? Did he have the right to fight for Tosh? He swallowed down another whiskey and watched the screen. Hamish was right. What's not to like about a kick-ass raccoon?

* * * *

Standing beside Hamish's car the next evening, Sam pulled his brother into his arms. "I wish you were closer."

Hamish opened the car door. "I've been pondering moving back here for a while. Stirling is nice, but I miss the sea, and I miss messing about in boats. I used to love helping out on the Seascape II in the summer. Maybe, if I can find a job locally…"

"That would be brilliant. You always did love going out on the water with the Sea Scouts as well. I remember those knots you used to be able to do. Can you still do a sheepshank?"

Hamish grinned. "Oh yeah, I can do a sheepshank, and I've learned lots of new knots since I was a scout."

Hamish's raised eyebrows gave Sam the impression his brother's sex life was even more interesting than he'd disclosed.

As Sam watched his brother drive away, he missed him already. His phone bleeped in his pocket. After removing it, he saw the text was from Tosh.

Dad doing OK. Will be back next week. See you Wed night at YC.

Well, it was better than nothing.

Chapter Sixteen

Sam had just finished putting out the chairs and tables when Cameron and Tosh walked in. He squashed the feelings of jealousy that surfaced when he saw them together.

"There are quite a few kids out there," Cameron said. "Should I let them in?"

"I don't see why not. We've the screen set up, and a dartboard. One of the locals gave us the table football, and Mrs. M has volunteered to show anyone who's interested how to decorate cupcakes. I expect many of them will simply be glad to get away from home and out of the rain."

Twenty-five students came into the hall and settled down in various places. More than he'd expected chose to go through to the kitchen area, where Mrs. McPherson had set out lots of small sponges ready to be iced and decorated with lots of sprinkles. Each one sat around the table, trying to work out how to use piping bags and add colors. Sam hoped they wouldn't make too much of a mess, but Mrs. McPherson kept them in line. Ally had returned and was currently swirling various colors on top of a cupcake, making a rainbow effect. Sam couldn't help overhearing their conversation.

"Those are lovely, dear. Rainbows are so pretty."

Ally tensed. "The rainbows represent the LGBTQIA groupings," she said, sticking out her chin. Sam recognized a challenge when he saw one. Obviously Ally expected a negative comment from the older person sitting next to her. Instead, Mrs. McPherson continued icing her bun and smiled.

"I know they do, dearie. I may be in my seventies, but I'm not blind to the changes in society. I'm pleased the laws have changed for the better. I wish it could have come sooner."

"Really, Mrs. M., I thought you'd be lecturing me on God and sin and being damned. You know I'm gay, don't you?"

Sam loved Ally's honesty and envied it. If a sixteen-year-old girl could be honest with herself, and others, then maybe… He was about to walk away and leave them to it, but was curious to hear Mrs. McPherson's reply.

"Yes, Ally. Your grandmother told me about it when we had tea in Maggie's Café a few weeks back, and I think you've been brave telling people. Your granny was shocked and worried for your future, but I told her you were exactly the same person she'd always loved, and she *does* love you."

She patted Ally's hand as the young woman wiped away a tear. "Now, none of that. I had a son, you see. His name was Malachi. His father insisted on it. I say *was*, because I've no idea if he's still alive." Sam noticed she hadn't let go of Ally's hand. He had no idea Mrs. M had ever had a son, only a nasty brute of a husband, who had thankfully died before Sam had been appointed. His reputation as a bigot was well known. If Mr. McPherson had still been among the elders now, Sam had no doubt he would've been removed if he had revealed his sexuality.

Ally turned to face the older lady as the others continued making a mess, oblivious to the conversation. "What happened to him? "Ally asked.

"He told us he was a homosexual on his eighteenth birthday. My husband threw him out of the house and told him never to darken our door again. He wouldn't even let me hug my son goodbye. The words he used and the names he called our child are etched into my memory."

"And you've no idea what happened to him?"

"No, he'd be in his mid-fifties now. So, you see, be glad you can be so open, and don't let anyone make you hide who you are. I wish I'd have been able to do more, but back then, I had nothing and nowhere to go. I couldn't leave my husband. You embrace your life, and don't let anyone tell you not to be who you are. Some woman will be lucky to have you. Now, let's get back to seeing what sort of mess this lot are making, shall we?"

Sam wiped a tear from his eye. He turned to see Cameron and Tosh playing table football with a couple of the lads. Others sat around, staring intently at their phones, or throwing darts without much success. He jumped at a tap on his shoulder and pivoted to see Gus behind him.

"He's a handsome bloke, Cameron."

"Yes, I suppose he is."

"But you weren't watching him, were you?"

Once again, Sam wondered if his brother had Jedi mind-reading skills. "No," he whispered.

"Is something up between you and Tosh? I noticed you haven't spoken to each other tonight."

Sam stared across the room to where Tosh and Cameron were noisily high-fiving each other. "We had words. I'm not sure how the land lies after his father's heart attack. I did something stupid."

"I'm guessing it may have involved Cameron."

Sam glanced around. "This isn't the best place to talk with so many ears available to listen. I keep thinking he'd be better off with the likes of Cameron."

His determination to fight for Tosh had faded, seeing him and Cameron together, especially as Tosh hadn't said two words to him since he'd arrived.

"Okay, but don't do anything stupid in the meantime. I know what you're like." Gus strolled over to the dartboard. For a moment, Tosh glanced in his direction, but Sam lowered his gaze and returned to the kitchen.

Around nine-thirty, Tosh headed out of the door with Cameron. Sam wanted to go and drag Tosh back, to hold his face in his hands and kiss him forever, to feel his body against his own, to breathe in his scent, but instead, he stared and said nothing.

"You just going to give up, then?" Gus said when they were alone.

"I don't know. I have so much baggage and Tosh deserves—"

"You," Gus stated. "You know he kept glancing over at you all night. D'you think he might have been deliberately trying to make you jealous?"

"But why?"

"I don't know. You said you'd done something stupid. Maybe this is payback. We can all be childish at times and sometimes we want the other person to make an effort. Take some advice from an old married man."

Sam smiled for the first time that evening. "I suppose you may have a point. I'll go round tomorrow."

"Good, now let's sort this place out."

With Gus' help, he tidied everything away before locking up and getting into his car. He turned down Gus' offer to come back to his and Mel's house, intending to go home and pour himself a few glasses of whiskey before retiring to his bed, alone, as he'd been for so long before Tosh. His phone bleeped. He stared at the message. Tosh was the last person he'd expected to contact him.

Come round to mine after 11 tonight. The key will be under the white pot by the back door. I'll be waiting.

Sam read the words three times to make sure. What was going on? Not that it mattered, because he knew where he'd be at the appointed time, whatever the outcome.

* * * *

"You do realize this could backfire spectacularly, don't you? What if he doesn't turn up?"

Tosh sighed. Cameron could be right, and Tosh wasn't the sort of person who played games, but he'd been hurt at Sam's lack of trust, and the truth was that he needed someone to talk to—someone who wasn't Darach—and who didn't have the baggage of a shared history. He hadn't told Cameron everything, but Sam's work situation was enough of an issue to be going on with. Tosh wasn't prepared to go into the closet for long, but equally, he wanted Sam to make the decision for himself, not because Tosh would be his reward. Bloody hell, relationships were complicated. Maybe that was why he and Harry had been so perfect—no dramas.

"If he doesn't turn up, then I know he's put the church first, and I have to accept that, and we haven't gone so far along not to be able to break up."

"Really? You sound so matter-of-fact."

Tosh held out his quivering hand. He picked up the whiskey glass with the other. "And that's why I suggested we pop in here for a quick drink before you took me home. This is Dutch courage. If he turns up, I have activities in mind I want us to try."

"So you and he haven't…?"

"It's complicated."

"These things often are."

"What about you, Cameron? What brought you here? I know about your family but…"

"I came because there was a job. When my parents threw me out, I moved in with my older sister in Inverness. She lives there with her partner, Ewan, and their two kids. She took me in and I found out Dad wouldn't speak to her either, because she was living in sin. So now they've lost both of their children and their grandchildren. I think Mum wants to see me. We've talked a few times on the phone, but she won't go against Dad."

Tosh gazed up and offered a quick 'thank you' for his parents who, despite their religious beliefs, put him first. "I'm so lucky. Has there been anyone special in your life, or am I prying too much?"

"No one who mattered. There was a lad when I was young, but we only messed about—nothing serious. And who'd want to put up with me being a teacher now, with our stupid hours? Talking of which, I should get off soon. I've a pile of designs to go through before tomorrow. I can't say the dog ate them, now can I? Seeing as I don't have a dog."

"Okay, give me a lift home, and I can get ready to see if Sam turns up."

"Sounds exciting. I'm imagining all sorts."

Tosh winked. "That's for me to know and you to speculate." He swallowed the rest of his whiskey.

Tosh glanced around when they pulled up in front of his house. Cameron leaned across and pulled him into a hug.

"Good luck, Tosh. I hope it works out for you."

"Me too. And thanks for tonight. You've been a good friend."

"Well, you know where I am if it all goes pear-shaped."

Tosh climbed out of the car and waved as Cameron drove away. He wiped rain from his face, pushed the key in the lock and checked along the road again, but all was silent except for the plinking of the rain and the sound of the waves hitting the shingle on the beach. Not even a dog-walker had braved the gloom this late at night. He turned the key and closed the door behind him.

From farther down the street, Sam watched the two men hug. Had Tosh brought him here to see them? But Cameron hadn't gone inside with Tosh, and to be fair, Sam had arrived earlier than Tosh had said to be there. The light disappeared in the living room. Had Tosh gone upstairs? Would he be waiting for him there? The sudden vision of Tosh lying naked on the bed, stroking himself, filled Sam's mind and his treacherous cock responded immediately. He wanted to be there. He wanted to touch Tosh, to hear him, to smell him, to taste him. Oh, God, he wanted to taste him, all salty on his tongue. Hamish was right, he deserved to be loved like anyone else, didn't he?

The key was exactly where Tosh had said it would be. Sam turned it slowly in the lock, pushed open the back door then secured it behind him. Unsure whether to switch on the light, he remained in the dark and carefully navigated his way through the kitchen and main room to the bottom of the stairs. He placed his hand on the bannister to steady himself and hoped his legs would manage to carry him upstairs toward the strip of light shining from under the room he knew to be Tosh's bedroom. Counting to himself, he climbed each step until he stood in front of the door. Should he say something? He hadn't been quiet so Tosh must have heard him.

"Come in, Sam. I know you're there. I've been waiting for you."

A thousand butterflies beat their wings in his stomach as he tried to swallow and wet his throat. He edged his shaking hand nearer the handle and pressed it down. In his head, his imagination returned to the image of Tosh lying there, naked on his bed, stroking his cock as he had been the last time he'd opened his door late at night. That vision was dashed as soon as he stepped into the room. Instead, Tosh was sitting up in bed, Kindle in one hand, glasses perched on the end of his nose, reading. The vision was all too ordinary, and so much better than the one he'd had in his mind before he'd entered the room. Tosh put down the Kindle and smiled at him.

"You decided to come, then. I wasn't sure if you would."

Sam let out a long breath. "I wasn't sure I would, either." He needed to say something. "Are you reading anything good?" He wanted to kick himself for asking the inanest question he'd ever asked anyone in his life. He shifted from foot to foot. "I'm sorry, I'm not sure what to do. Half of me expected you to be lying there naked, hard and needy."

Tosh's cheeks flushed. His soft brown eyes shone like pools of liquid chocolate reflecting the light from the lamp. What the fuck? Since when did he use words like those to describe anyone's eyes?

"I nearly was, but it seemed too...blatant. And you know what it's like reading Terry Pratchett. One chapter leads to another and another. I've been putting it off because there won't be any more. So sad what happened to him."

"Yes, it was. Dementia is such a terrible condition."

"Darach's mum has it. I hate seeing her getting worse. Such a vital force fading bit by bit. It's tearing him apart."

If Sam had expected any conversation when he'd entered the room, it wasn't this one.

"It makes you realize how little time we might have in this world, and how we should live every day. Losing Harry taught me that much. Come over here. You look like you're going to fall down at any minute. I promise I won't bite."

Sam closed the distance between them and sat at the end of Tosh's bed. "I know how fragile life can be," he said quietly.

"So what are we going to do with this knowledge we have about life and its uncertainties?"

"Hamish came to see me over the weekend. We talked. I appear to have two choices — I can throw caution to the wind and follow my heart..."

"Or?"

"I can tell you I'll love you always, but you don't deserve to get tied down with a reckless coward like me who could kill you."

"Really? Is that the best you can do?"

"It seemed to fit."

"I did wonder if you were deliberately trying to push me toward Cameron."

"Well, he's young, good-looking and smart and..." He hesitated. "And he's clean."

Any inkling of humor on Tosh's face disappeared instantly. "Is that how you see yourself? As unclean? Should someone be ringing a bell in front of you?" He seized Sam's face in both hands. "How I hate that word. You are not dirty. You were unlucky, that's all. Like so many others. It isn't a judgment."

"Isn't it? Lots of people would disagree with you."

"Shit happens. Bad things happen to good people and

138

good things happen to bad people. Look at all those dodgy lottery winners. Oh, God, Sam, you think you don't deserve love or happiness. That this is your cross to bear, and it's fucking nonsense. You are a good man. When Harry died, I was lost and drifting, but you anchored me and somehow sneaked under my defenses. I didn't see you at first, only the collar, but then something would happen and I'd want to tell you about it, and hear you laugh, making your oh-so-solemn face crease with lines."

"But it's so complicated."

"Fuck that," Tosh replied, taking Sam's hand into his own.

"Tosh."

"I'm sorry for the language, but I understand how short life is. My life was taken away without warning. Harry's death wasn't God's judgement any more than what happened to Brice. I don't want Cameron. I want the man sitting in front of me who has just said he loves me, in case you've forgotten. I want you even with this awful beard."

Sam ran his fingers across his chin. "Do you really think it's horrible?"

Tosh's smile turned into laughter until tears flowed down his face. Relief washed over Sam and he found himself joining in and laughing.

"Sometimes you need your arse slapped with the rubbish you come out with," Tosh managed between wiping the damp from his cheeks.

"I thought I'd put it out there. I want you to be sure."

"You mentioned making a decision earlier." Tosh leaned forward. "So which choice did you decide to follow? I'm hoping for the first, and that you've decided to throw caution to the wind."

"And risk everything?" Sam hesitated for a moment. "I wasn't sure until I heard Ally talking to Mrs. M at the youth club tonight, before I got your text. And I had to be sure about Cameron."

"Oh for fuck's sake. Shut up and kiss me." Tosh shifted

on the bed, moving nearer to him. Sam met him halfway, and their lips touched. He allowed Tosh to wrap his arms around him and drag him down until he lay on top. He kissed anywhere he could reach.

"Oh, God, Tosh, I've missed you so much. Yes, please, I need...more."

Tosh had thrust his hands inside Sam's jeans and briefs to cup his arse and press them together. Tosh's hardness mirrored his own.

"Too many clothes," Tosh whispered.

Sam moved back until he was straddling Tosh's legs. He pulled off his shirt, leaving the buttons.

Tosh wet a single finger and ran it down the center of Sam's chest, following the trail of hair to the waistband of his jeans.

"It's funny how you're the lone blond among your brothers. I used to wonder if you dyed it to be different from them, but now I can see it goes all the way down."

Deftly, Tosh undid Sam's zipper and pressed his hand against the bulge straining to be freed. "I'm aware of what you and I face, Sam. If your viral load is undetectable then the risk is small, and if we do make a mistake, there's something I can take, a bit like the Morning After Pill. I'm a grown-up, capable of making my own decisions about the risks I take with my body."

"But what if I'm not prepared to do anything to put you at risk, no matter what my status and viral load? I know what the studies say. Do you think I haven't read about PrEP? They even mentioned using it on *How to Get Away with Murder*. I still couldn't bear to be responsible for infecting you."

"If we're careful, there's no need to worry."

"Accidents happen, Tosh. I can't. No matter how slight the danger is. I may not be on message, and maybe I'll change my mind in the future. Not all men fuck. I'll understand if that means..."

Tosh placed a finger on his mouth. "Do you think I'm so

140

shallow I'd drop you because you don't want to fuck for now? There's a lot of future in front of us, and they make medical advances all the time."

"No, but it's more important to some people than others."

Tosh shifted to a sitting position with his back resting against the padded headboard. "Open the second drawer, will you. I want you to choose which and who."

Puzzled, Sam reached over to the handle, trying not to overbalance. He dragged it open.

"Shit! Are they what I think they are?"

"Yep. I thought we might find a use for one or more of them."

Sam ran his fingers over the contents of the drawer and chose two. "This one is so smooth." He held it up to the light. "The myriad blues are stunning, like the sea's ever-changing hue as clouds roll over it." He placed the dildo on the bed beside him. "And this one." He ran his fingers over the ridged surface to the more pronounced head.

"It's extraordinary someone made this with so many colors swirling around." How did he admit he'd never owned a dildo for fear his cleaner would find it? "I mean I knew they existed, but I've never seen one made of glass. They are astonishing. I can't stop touching this one, and it's warming in my hand. It felt cold to begin with but now…"

"I hope you don't think it's weird, but I got the idea from Harry. He has a collection of antique ones."

"Harry collected glass dildos?"

Tosh's cheeks flushed red again. "Yes, he did. They're packed away now, even though they are truly beautiful pieces of sculpture. These two are modern examples I bought recently. He said they'd be collectables in the future. I keep them in the trunk over there. Some are more than a hundred years old. I've thought of displaying them in here…but maybe that would be weird."

Sam touched his arm. "They mattered to you. Did you and Harry…?"

"Sometimes. Does that matter? I'll understand if it does.

I just wanted to be able to give you the pleasure and the feeling is wonderful."

Did it matter to him? He kissed Tosh then picked up the nearest example. He stroked the smooth surface again, tracing the lines of blue with one finger. He longed to see Tosh writhing under him. He glanced up to see Tosh watching his hand.

"Watching you touching one has lessened the room in my shorts. The thought of easing it slowly into your arse..."

Sam tensed. "You want to fuck me with it. I thought..."

"I have more than one, Sam. We could fuck each other with either, depending on which you prefer."

Sam shivered from head to toe. If he couldn't push himself into Tosh, he could at least see him opened up, and touch him. He desperately wanted to taste him on his tongue. Sam glanced up at Tosh's face which had flushed again.

"What?"

"I may have prepared before you came. They don't only make dildos in glass."

Sam swallowed hard. "Show me," he whispered.

Tosh pulled back the duvet. "Pull them off me." He lifted his arse off the bed so Sam could remove his boxers.

Sam grasped either side of the shorts and dragged them down before flinging them on the floor. He waited, dampening his lips as Tosh opened his legs and lifted his knees to reveal a wider black glass base sticking out of his arse in vivid contrast to his white skin covered in dark downy hair. His cock stood proud among the trimmed curls.

Sam leaned back and stared, a hand on each thigh, his cock straining for release. He wished he could take hold of himself and cover Tosh with his cum, mark him as his own.

"You're staring," Tosh said.

"Sorry, but you might be the most incredible sight I've ever seen."

"Me, nah. I'm just a flabby, pale-skinned postman with a butt plug up my arse. Tell you what—choose one."

Sam picked up the smooth piece of glass all concerns about their use now gone.

Tosh turned to his side and propped himself up on his elbow. "Lie on your back next to me."

Sam did as he was told, waiting as Tosh retrieved a tube from the drawer and handed it to him.

"Prep yourself. I want to watch, then I'm going to fuck you with this."

Sam's arse flexed at the thought. He could do this. He raised his legs and bit by bit pushed one, then two, then three fingers inside, feeling the burn, the stretch, pressing down to make it easier until he was full, both aroused and embarrassed by how exposed he felt under Tosh's gaze. Tosh's eyes widened at the sight and became almost completely black. When Tosh licked his lips, Sam's cock stiffened more than he thought possible.

Worried that he might come there and then, he withdrew his fingers. "I'm ready, Tosh. Fuck me, please."

Tosh smiled as he covered the glass in lube. "You don't need as much," he explained. "But I'll make sure."

"You won't hurt me. Unlike that, I'm not made of glass." He held out his hand, needing Tosh to touch him. The glass was cool against his skin. He bore down as Tosh slowly sank the dildo into him until the slight turn at the head touched his prostate, and he jerked. "Oh yeah, just there."

Tosh moved to kneel between Sam's legs and fucked him. "I'm leaking," Sam said, tensing. "Cover me with a condom, just in case. I want to be safe. I want you to be safe."

"All right. We do what you want."

Tosh passed Sam the unwrapped condom and waited while he rolled it over his erection before maneuvering himself until he straddled Sam's chest. He squeezed lube on his hand and stroked himself.

Oh, God, he was so close. Sam wanted to suck him.

Tosh shifted forward and tapped Sam's mouth with his cock, allowing a drop or two of pre-cum to touch his lips. Sam stuck out his tongue to get a taste.

"Oh, God, I wish," Sam muttered.

"There's very little risk," Tosh said. "Open up. Let me rest it on your tongue."

Sam couldn't help himself. His need was overcoming his fear. Tosh was right. He parted his lips and stuck out his tongue. Tosh fed his cock into Sam's waiting mouth. He closed his lips around the shaft and let Tosh control everything, let him fuck his mouth while he hummed. Then panic hit him and he stopped.

"All right?" Tosh asked, withdrawing.

"Touch yourself. I want to watch you. Tell me when you're ready. Come on my face, and I can lick you off my lips."

"Jeez, Sam, if I get any harder, I'll be able to drill through steel." He fisted his cock, hurrying himself to a finish.

"So close."

His stroke rate increased until he moaned, sending streams of hot liquid over Sam's face and into his open mouth. Sam tasted Tosh on his tongue and licked his lips before he reached behind Tosh and grasped his own cock, knowing it wouldn't take long.

"Watch me," he said. "Watch my face."

Tosh's gaze didn't leave his as he arched his body and came into the condom, his arse contracting around the dildo with the curve pressing on his prostate. It was perfect. In his head, his body was full of Tosh. Eventually, he could stand no more and withdrew the smooth glass to put it to one side, before he collapsed back onto the bed, gasping for breath.

"Bloody hell," Tosh said above him. "Have you any idea how hot it was seeing you coming with my spunk still over your face?"

"I need to get rid of the condom," Sam said, afraid of spoiling the moment.

Tosh leaned over and picked up the bin. Sam carefully removed the rubber and tied it off then placed it in the bin. Tosh swiftly extracted his own plug, grabbed a wipe and cleaned Sam's face.

"Lie down and I'll snuggle in around you."

Sam couldn't remember being so happy in his life and wriggled closer when Tosh wrapped an arm around his waist, laying his palm on Sam's stomach. Sam held Tosh's hand in his own. Behind him, Tosh sighed, letting out a long, slow breath. Sam clutched Tosh's fingers.

"Sam?"

"Yes."

"You know what you said earlier when you had your *Bodyguard* moment? Did you mean it?"

Sam tried not to tense, and failed. "What? About me leaving if you want me to?" His mouth dried and he swallowed hard, afraid of what was coming next. He turned his face to the pillow. *Please don't let him say he wants me to go. Not now. Not after what we've just done. In the morning. Maybe I could bear it in the morning.*

"No, not that." Tosh squeezed his hand tighter. "I meant the bit about you always loving me, because I think I might love you too."

Sam opened his mouth, but no words came out. Tosh pressed his head closer. His breathing slowed and evened out until Sam guessed he was asleep. He couldn't lose this man. Whatever the consequences, he needed to tell everyone the truth.

Chapter Seventeen

"Were they really okay when you told them?"

Tosh sighed. He'd already reviewed the conversation he'd had with his parents earlier in the day twice. "Yes, I've told you virtually word for word what they said."

"Even though I'm a Church of Scotland minister?"

"Yes, though you're tall and blond, have a beard and appear awesomely sexy in a long black ministerial robe, even if you don't wear it that often… And yes, before you check again, they won't say anything to anyone before you do. They're my parents and they love me. Mum says each person must find their own path to God. Anyway, your lot are more likely to get upset about the smirch of popery. So can we give it a rest now? I'm nervous enough going to have dinner with your family already."

"But they know you."

"That may well be true, but they know me as the postman, not the man sleeping with their son or brother. It changes things, and you said your parents had been quiet since you told them I was the someone." It had been a couple of days since Sam had finally shared the information with his parents, so last night, Tosh had sat his own parents down and explained about Sam. It had gone better than he'd expected. Sam's mum had phoned that morning to ask them both for dinner but that was all. Tosh couldn't help feeling concerned.

"I don't think they're worried about *you*. Not in that way. I think they might be more worried *for* you. It's not as if you've seduced me into a life of perversion, is it?"

Sam slowed the car and found a space in the busy street.

"Hopefully, everyone should be there by now, as we're late. I know we could have had dinner with one brother at a time, but I thought it would be easier to appear as a couple and get everything out of the way at the same time. Grab the flowers and whiskey from the back, will you?"

Tosh did as he was told and climbed out of the passenger seat. He glanced from side to side, but the street was quiet in the steadily falling rain.

"Come on," Sam said, giving him a devastating smile. "It's now or never."

Tosh straightened his back and stood tall. He'd made an effort to dress well in black trousers and a proper shirt. Sam, having come straight from the service to pick him up, was still wearing black, accessorized with a pale blue tie rather than his dog collar. The front door opened and Sam's eldest brother, Alec, filled the space. Tosh guessed his welcoming smile was meant to reassure him as Tosh persuaded his legs to walk up the path.

Alec hugged Sam as soon as they were through the door, then Alec turned to Tosh.

"It's good to have you here, Tosh. Everyone's arrived. I know it's going to be daunting having you here, given the circumstances, and joining a family like ours is nothing short of intimidating, but you know us all."

If Alec hoped his words would reassure Tosh, he was wrong. Despite the coolness of the day, beads of sweat had formed on his brow.

"I…" His throat had dried so much he croaked out the first word. "Sorry, dry mouth. I guess I'm nervous about what's through the door."

Alec slung an arm around him. "I remember the first time I met Sandie's parents. I'm a butcher and they're professional architects. They designed and built their own house. Sandie and I wouldn't have moved in the same circles except for her treading in the cow pat at the Turriff show, and me coming to her rescue. Going into her amazing house, I was more scared than I've ever been in my life.

We're on your side, you know. If you're prepared to take on a Carmichael brother, you're all right with us. Come on then, deep breath."

Tosh followed the brothers through the door into the main living room, and five heads lifted to stare in their direction. One by one, each person smiled. When Sam squeezed his hand, Tosh didn't want to let go.

"You know everyone here already," Sam said. "Mum and Sandie in the kitchen, then?"

Tosh stepped toward Sam's father. "I brought you this, sir. Sam said it was your favorite." He handed over the whiskey.

"It's good to have you here, Tosh. Why don't you sit? Lunch won't be long. Sam's mother has been fussing over it for hours now making sure the beef is cooked properly."

"That's the best beef anyone could eat," Alec said. "I chose it myself and I could tell you its name, but I know some people are sensitive about that sort of thing." Alec stared directly at Gus.

"What?" Gus said. "Darach's the same. His family always know which pig they're eating."

Tosh grinned. He'd had many a dinner at the McNaughton farm. "I remember how they used to tease him about becoming a vegetarian, but he couldn't give up bacon."

Both Alec and his father shivered. Gordon Carmichael stared at his youngest son then turned back to Tosh. "Vegetarian is a swear word in this house, son."

Aisling rose from the sofa. "I'll get a vase for those flowers, shall I? They'll sit lovely on the windowsill." She touched Tosh's shoulder as she passed. "It's good to have you here, Tosh. He needs someone like you with a sensible head on your shoulders. They all do, the Carmichael men. They may not always switch their brains on before they open their mouths to speak, but their hearts are in the right place, and they are loyal to a fault. Hurt one, and you hurt them all."

Was that a veiled warning? Tosh didn't think so. He'd

been in the same year as Aisling in school. "I know," he whispered. "I'll never do anything to hurt him."

Aisling patted his arm once more and disappeared into the kitchen briefly. Tosh stood for a moment, unsure what to do until Aisling returned and announced they should sit at the large table at the other end of the long lounge. Light streamed in from the French doors as the sun emerged from behind a cloud and illuminated the garden at the back of the terrace.

Tosh took the seat in the middle with Sam on his left, and Mel and Gus on his right. Opposite sat Aisling, Stuart and Alec. The kitchen door swung open, and Sandie pushed through carrying a large piece of roast beef on a platter surrounded by roast potatoes. The smell made Tosh's mouth water. Sandie placed the joint in front of Sam's father, who raised a large knife to sharpen it on the steel before cutting slices for everyone and handing each of them plates.

One by one, Sandie brought in bowls of vegetables and a plate of Yorkshire puddings, until Mrs. Carmichael came in with a large and wonderfully aromatic gravy boat. She placed it in front of them and sat at the other end of the table.

Tosh waited. Would they say grace? His mother still did at every meal. He got his answer straight away.

"Tuck in, everyone. We don't stand on ceremony here."

Sam squeezed his knee.

"This looks so lovely, Mrs. Carmichael," Tosh said, hoping his hands weren't shaking so much he'd drop a roast potato on the beautiful lace tablecloth.

"Call me Gill. The girls do. It's good to have you here, Tosh. How are your parents? I hear your father's been ill but is on the mend now."

"Yes, he's been told to take it easy and change his lifestyle, but the doctors did a good job on his heart. Mum's fussing, of course, and will drive him mad supervising his diet. This meat is so wonderful. My dad would be envious now he's been told to eat less red meat."

"Bloody nonsense. Didn't do me any harm."

Tosh glanced at Gordon Carmichael. He remained a strapping figure of a man with huge shoulders and arms, no doubt from lugging around carcasses. His graying hair was now shredded through with all the shades of red he'd handed on to four of his sons. Sam had bucked the trend and inherited his dark blond locks from his mother. He picked up a piece of beef and placed it on his tongue, where it practically melted. After swallowing, he smiled.

"I think if Dad ever tasted beef as good as this, Mum might have to tie him down to stop him from eating it."

The chuckle from one brother shifted to each in turn and finally turned to laughter. Stuart leaned toward his mother while gazing at his father and winking. "I told you he had a way with words, didn't I? Quite the charmer is Brodie Mackintosh. No wonder our Sam couldn't resist him and his other attributes."

The laughing stopped and Tosh froze, uncertain of what might be said next.

"And once again my husband proves he can occasionally be a good judge of character, as well as beefcake."

"I didn't mean..." Stuart spluttered. "I don't..."

"Oh, for goodness sake, Stuart, put food in your mouth instead of your foot. I'm sorry about my son, Tosh. As a mother, you try to bring your children up exactly the same."

Gill Carmichael reached an arm around her second son, as did his wife. "It's a good job we love him anyway, and he did find a sensible woman to marry him."

"It's not fair," Stuart said. "I'm being picked on."

"Now you know how I feel," Gus said. "Being the youngest of five was—no, is—a nightmare. It's a shame Hamish isn't here. He'd love having us together. Have you told him?"

Tosh relaxed at the change of topic and winked at Stuart, who was still pretending to be hurt by the family banter.

"Hamish knows. He said he'd try to get up here next

holiday if work allows."

Tosh spent the rest of the afternoon listening to stories only families could tell on each other, of injuries caused from fights, either real or playing, of illnesses they'd had and who was the worst as Tosh heard of all the places each of them had managed to get chicken pox.

"At least you didn't get them up your arse like Hamish did," Alec said when his mother had left the room to bring out the dessert.

Tosh shifted in his seat at the thought. "I managed to avoid those childhood ailments. Must be from not having any siblings. I thought the kids might be here as well today."

Sandie looked to the skies. "We've left them with a couple of babysitters. It takes two to manage them. We thought it was better if there were no distractions today. But don't worry, you'll get your chance to babysit if you play your cards right."

Tosh glanced around nervously. "I've never had any dealings with taking care of children."

"Except helping one come into the world," Sam said proudly.

"Susie did the work, not me. I don't know how women do it."

At that moment, their mother came into the room with a huge cheesecake covered in strawberries. "I don't know. Shelled them out like peas around here. But five was enough. And I ended up with wonderful daughters, anyway."

"Aye, son, it was awful here when they were youngsters. If one of them came down with something they all did. Fairly wore their mother out when they succumbed to a stomach bug. I was glad we put in an extra toilet downstairs, and even that wasn't enough sometimes."

"Gordon, do we have to? I don't think Tosh wants to hear you discussing the need for a toilet while eating." Mrs. Carmichael put the huge dish on the table with a large jug of cream. She cut each of them a portion.

Despite Sam's mother's comment, Tosh was regaled

with more stories of childhood accidents and games that had nearly had disastrous consequences as they ate the magnificent pie. Finally, she gave in and joined the conversation.

"And the noise levels. Sometimes now, with only me and Gordon here, it's too quiet, but then we do have the grandchildren to take care of, and they seem to be following their fathers for the amount of noise they can make." She stood to pick up the now empty dishes. "I'll make tea for everyone, and you can help me wash up, Tosh."

Tosh glanced at Sam, searching for a way out of this request, but Sam shrugged while the others grinned. Mel nudged him. "We've all been through it," she whispered.

He swallowed hard and gathered the rest of the plates. "Of course, Mrs. Carmichael. It would be my pleasure." He hoped his hands weren't shaking so much he'd drop the crockery on the floor.

Once in the kitchen, Mrs. Carmichael donned her apron and stood in front of the sink. "I'll wash and you dry. Stack everything there, and we'll put it away afterwards."

Tosh picked up the tea towel and stood, waiting. It didn't take long for the interrogation to begin.

"Sam says you've told your parents about you and him. Have you told them everything?"

"No, not the HIV, but they know Sam and I are in a relationship."

"Is that what they call it these days? Well, I suppose you're hardly going out together, are you? I've never liked secrets."

"Being secret is Sam's choice, not mine."

"And you're ready for what might happen, all the comments you're going to get, and even the downright hostility. Some people might think you've led him away from the light."

Tosh carefully placed the plate on the pile. "Is that what you think?"

"No, Gordon and I aren't religious. When Sam announced

his intention to become a minister, we were shocked. The boys hadn't been taken to church by us. Sam toddled off with his granny sometimes, and maybe she influenced him. We haven't told her anything yet, but I suppose he's going to have to face her sometime. It'll be hard for him, as he was always my mother's favorite. And you're a Catholic, aren't you?"

"I was brought up a Catholic, yes, but I disagree with too much of what they purport to be true." Where the hell was this conversation going?

"I liked Harry, your…"

"Husband," Tosh provided.

"Yes, your partner."

Tosh noted the unsubtle change of wording. "I liked him too."

"What happened…so shocking. I have no words that would be adequate. These things take time to get over, and I don't want Sam to get hurt. I don't want him to declare himself to everyone if you're not certain, if he's a rebound relationship with no meaning. Do you love him? I've seen the way he gazes at you like you're his favorite sort of chocolate, and a mother knows. He loves you."

Tosh wiped the last of the dishes and placed it on the counter. This was a question he could answer.

"Well, do you?"

"Yes, I love him."

"Enough to take chances with your own health?"

"Sam wouldn't put me at risk. I do know I don't want to lose him. He's my friend and anyway, I don't think he's coming out for me. He's decided to tell the truth about himself for his own good, to stop living a lie, even if it costs him his job. There are plenty of other places that would take him, gay or not, and the church voted to allow ministers in a same-sex partnership as long as the congregation agreed."

"I had hopes, you see. The same hopes I have for all my boys, that they would find a nice girl, settle down and give me lots of grandchildren. And he had girlfriends."

"But none of them were real, Mum."

Tosh turned at the sound of Sam's voice.

"And I could still have children if my partner wants them."

Tosh raised his eyebrows when his gaze met Sam's scrutiny. He and Harry had planned to have children.

Sam's expression softened. "I'm sorry to interrupt, but I figured you'd had enough time to talk by now, and Mum, he's right. I'm not coming out because of him, although I'd be lying if I didn't say he helped me to make the decision. I'm fed up with lying to everyone when they ask when I'm going to find a nice girl to settle down. Tosh didn't give me any ultimatums, and we're both aware that we have a lot of baggage to deal with if this relationship is going to work. But we're both totally committed to making a go of things, aren't we?"

Tosh saw the plea in those blue eyes. Could he give Sam up now? Did he want to go back to his lonely existence? Harry would have wanted him to be happy, and Sam made him happy. Despite the issues and problems, he'd rather be with Sam than without, whatever the cost. The thought smacked him between the eyes. He closed the gap between them, and clasped Sam's hands in his own.

"I don't want to lose you. I'm here for you whatever happens. I couldn't have survived the last eighteen months without you."

Sam pulled him into a hug, his mouth next to Tosh's ear. "That's all I needed to hear."

The sound of the kettle boiling brought them out of their bubble. Sam let him go and crossed the floor to where his mother stood wiping away tears from her cheeks. Tosh lifted the kettle and filled the two large teapots, while Sam hugged his mother. She appeared so small next to him. He placed everything on the large tray and left them to it.

Whatever happened over the next few weeks, Sam's family would be there for him, and he would be right by Sam's side.

Chapter Eighteen

Sam paced in the back room of the church. "Maybe I should do my regular service after all. I'm worried I'm hijacking Matilda's christening."

Tosh grasped Sam's hand and stroked his wrist gently. Sam stared down at the movement.

"Darach says Brice strokes his wrist when he gets stressed, or has bad memories. It soothes him. Come on, breathe. The Moderator knows what you're doing and agreed it might be best to get everything out into the open. You were worried he'd tell you not to, but he didn't."

Sam shrugged. "I don't think he's against it, but I suspect he'd rather I didn't rock the boat. I told you the vote on LGBT issues has always been close in this area. But, if Cormac complains, and I've no doubt he will, at least the Moderator is prepared to organize a meeting."

"Is that what will happen?" Tosh asked. "I don't know how these things work."

"There's a Latin name for it. There will be the Moderator, ministers and elders from the Presbytery to vote and the congregation will be consulted, no doubt."

"But surely it won't matter in the end. You've brought people into the church, worked with the local schools and youth. That's got to count in your favor."

"It depends how vocal Cormac Campbell is."

"Well, Donny and Susie agreed to this. You do the christening, then give your sermon. After all, their daughter is being named after me. They told me they'd be proud to be part of you telling the world, and Matilda would be too, so this christening will be the start of two new lives. I'm going to slip out of the back and go round to the front of the church with the others. Remember, you're not going to be out there on your own. The place will be full of your family and friends. The christening has given them a reason to be here."

The door to the main part of the church opened and a man appeared. Sam's face lit up.

"Jock, you came. I'm so glad you're here. Is Joyce with you?"

"Of course. She's taken a seat. We wouldn't have missed this. I wanted to make sure you're all right. This is a bold move, but I suppose it gets it over with. No doubt anyone who isn't here will know by the end of the day, if I'm any judge of small town life. And you must be Brodie."

Sam stepped back as Jock stretched out his hand then pulled Tosh into a hug.

"Most people call me Tosh. Even Sam does now, though he held out for a while. I'm going to get off. Take care of him for me, will you? He's such a bundle of nerves that he's likely to forget how to do the christening service, and *I'm* a godparent."

"Don't worry. You go and take your place, and I'll stay with him. I made sure I brought my own robe just in case."

Tosh gave him a quick hug and kissed his cheek before disappearing out of the rear door. Jock closed the space between them and grasped his hand.

"You're sure you want to do this? It needs to be your decision and yours alone, not his, and not your family's. After you stand out there and tell everyone you're gay, your life is going to change. Some of them will accept who you are, and others will quote the Bible chapter and verse, declare you unclean and unfit to serve God or man. And if you and Tosh continue your relationship, people will soon find out. Until now, you've merely been helping him get over the death of his husband, and bringing him to the faith, but a few might say you took advantage of a bereaved man."

"Tosh and I have discussed his. We know it won't be easy, but we couldn't help falling in love."

"Is that what this is? Has he said he loves you?"

"Yes. I've not asked him for an announcement in the local paper, and we won't be moving in together. I'm a minister. I can't live in sin. The church has accepted same-sex marriage and partners, but we still have to set an example. I don't want to rush him, but I'd marry him tomorrow."

Jock patted Sam's hand. "You've got it bad, haven't you?"

Sam nodded. "I couldn't tell you exactly why, but he's the kindest, most level-headed person I've ever met. He makes me feel safe and excited at the same time, and I've never seen any pity in his eyes. He sees me, not my illness. I'm Sam first. If the people here don't accept me, and Tosh doesn't want to move anywhere else, then I'll give up the ministry."

"I see. Have you told him? It's a lot of pressure to put on him."

"No, let's get past today first."

The inner door opened, and Mrs. McPherson stepped in. "They're ready for you, Reverend."

Sam managed a slight smile then kissed the cross on his necklace before tucking it back inside his shirt. "Showtime," he said and followed Mrs. McPherson and Jock out.

Having a christening to do removed him from the safety of his pulpit. Instead of standing above the congregation, he now stood among them, at their level, in front of the small font. He welcomed everyone, noting many faces, some known and others new who weren't usually found sitting on the wooden pews. To his left, the elders sat on their own seats, and to his right, the organist sat at her instrument waiting for the nod to begin the first hymn. Sam was grateful for his long dark robes, which successfully covered his shaking knees. He placed his hands together, gripping tightly, nodded, and the introduction to the first hymn began.

The singing settled his nerves. He had a good voice, and

the extra numbers boosted the sound. Partway through, he glanced toward the back of the room. His brothers Alec and Stuart sat with their families. Gus sat with Mel. Next to them, Sam was surprised to see Darach. *He* certainly hadn't visited the church before.

With the song over, he called the McDougall family forward. The service wasn't an exact thing, so he mixed his own words with those necessary.

"Dear Father, thank you for this lovely day and for bringing everyone together in this place. Help us to walk in your footsteps in truth, in love and humility. Thank you for little Matilda Brodie here. Welcome her into your church. Help her parents and godparents to live up to their promises, and to tell her about Jesus. We pray in your name. Amen."

As he said the familiar words, Sam experienced a sensation of calm, even with Tosh standing behind the family. This was the third McDougall child he'd baptized into the church. True, they weren't regular attenders, but the church didn't require that of them. He lifted Matilda into his arms. She lay wrapped in the same shawl the McDougall family had used for years with its delicate lace made especially for an occasion like this, many decades ago.

He dipped his fingers into the water and placed the drips on her forehead. "I baptize you, Matilda Brodie McDougall, in the name of the Father, the Son and Holy Spirit."

As he continued the words, Matilda opened her mouth and wailed loudly enough to scare away any devil. Sam smiled down at her and pressed his little finger to her lips and she quieted. After asking the parents to bring her up in the faith, he turned to the congregation for the blessing and, as they sang, he knew he was getting nearer and nearer to confession time.

"Now, let us pray."

Once everyone had taken their seats, another hymn rang out around the small whitewashed building. He gazed into the distance, trying to remember the words he'd chosen to say. Maybe he should have written them down, but he wanted to show these words came from the heart, not from a well-practiced speech.

With the room silent again, except for the odd murmur from a small child, or cough from someone unable to stop themselves, he began.

"Today, we've welcomed Matilda into our church and congregation. As I look at her now with her family, her future is not known to us, but she is a bundle of possibilities. Along the way, she will receive help and advice from many, some she'll not want, but such is life. When I decided to become a minister, my parents were shocked. We weren't a religious family, and many of you may be surprised to see my brothers here among you. They're here to support me in the same way that Matilda's parents and godparents are here to support her. In the words of the baptism, I talked about truth, love and humility, and today, I'm going to share with you a truth. Some of you will find this difficult to hear. A few may feel I don't belong in these robes after all, and parts of the Bible will back you up, depending on how you read them. This year the Synod voted to allow gay, married ministers into the church, leading the way much as it did when they allowed women to become ministers many years ago."

He paused at the murmur of voices after his words, inhaled then exhaled slowly. "I believe God called me to be a minister, and I've never doubted or questioned my calling, even though for many years, I've not been fully honest with you about myself. Today that changes. There is one simple way to say this." He hesitated and breathed in, glancing around the space at the faces gazing at him. The silence was palpable. He needed to do this — say the words. "I'm gay. I stand before you as a gay man asking you to accept me, asking to continue as your minister, asking you to let me go on serving the people of this parish as I have done for the last six years."

A movement to his left made everyone turn. Sam wasn't

surprised to see Cormac Campbell standing, his face red with fury. "You cannae stay here. You're an abomination. That's what the Bible says. Man shall not lie with man. It's there in black and white. I don't care what the Synod says with its city ways, we don't want your sort here, do we?" He gazed at the people, waiting for an answer. No one stood, but there were a few nods and murmurs of agreement.

"And how dare you use the christening of an innocent child to announce your perversion," the elder continued.

Susie McDougall stood with Matilda still in her arms. "The reverend asked us if we would mind him speaking out today, and we were all for it. I'm a mother, like many of you in here. My children are precious to me. I love them unconditionally, exactly like I believe God does. If any of them turn out to be gay or transgender, I will love them the same because God created them. I'm proud Sam christened them all, and that Matilda is named after Brodie Mackintosh, who helped to bring her into the world. Thankfully, times change."

When Susie sat back on the pew, Mrs. McPherson rose from her seat. She was small and dressed conservatively in a green jumper and tartan skirt, but her presence always commanded respect.

"Jesus didn't mention homosexuality in any of his sermons." Mrs. McPherson spoke quietly but firmly. "He welcomed all people into his followers. I have attended this church since before I was old enough to stand. Many of you started coming here when the Reverend Carmichael came, especially the young people. He could have gone to any parish, but he chose to come home to work in the area where he was born, and I for one am glad. Jesus spoke about love, not hate, and that we love each other is all that matters." She paused. "And the Bible also says 'Let he who is without sin cast the first stone'. I've lived in this village for over seventy years, and I'm certainly a sinner."

Sam's eyes filled with tears at her words, but he brushed them aside. "We have a meeting of the kirk session next week.

I'm sure the elders will want to discuss my announcement, and I know this will have given many of you much to think upon. If anyone wants to talk to me individually, my door is always open."

He strode down the center aisle to the entrance and stood in his usual position to say goodbye to those who had attended. Some shook his hand, as usual. Others walked past, including the elder, Cormac Campbell, who'd spoken out earlier. A few, including Mrs. McPherson, hugged him and whispered their support. Finally, Tosh and his own family emerged. Tosh stood to one side, but his brothers surrounded him and patted him on the back.

"You did it," Alec said.

Sam nodded, unable to speak, unsure he had a voice. Tosh gave him the thumbs-up sign.

"Are you all right?" Aisling asked. "You've gone very pale."

A wave of tiredness threatened to overwhelm him until Jock appeared at his side and held his elbow. "I think you should go home, laddie," he said.

"Everyone, please come back with me. If the elders decide to get rid of me, at least we can have one last party at the manse." He mouthed 'you too' at Tosh and introduced him to Joyce.

* * * *

Sam stared out over his garden, shading his eyes from the sun shining out of a clear blue sky. Soon it would be autumn and the leaves would turn and fall, and the air become colder. Next would come harvest, then all the events leading up to Christmas, his favorite time of the year. The rose bushes growing on either side of the lawn gave off a perfume as they swayed in the gentle breeze, red and yellow and orange, blazing away against the cool green of the leaves and the white-washed walls. Behind him, his family ate and drank and laughed together, celebrating his coming out.

"I thought I might find you out here."

Sam turned at the familiar voice. "Sorry, Tosh. I needed a moment."

Tosh sat on the bench next to him. "I can go back in if you want. I've been talking to Jock and Joyce. I can see why he means so much to you. He's a fascinating man, and so passionate about the work he does with those kids."

"He saved me. I don't know what I would've done without him. When I was diagnosed, I thought my life was over. I was going to kill myself so I wouldn't be a burden to my family or anyone else. I couldn't see a future, but he showed me one and encouraged me to pray. I know you don't understand my faith, and how I can defend a belief system which condemns us, but I truly believe those words about love."

"I know you do. I want to be as certain as you, but I'm not. Maybe it was listening to Father McGuire when I was a child and all the talk of non-Catholics going to Hell. I don't know. All I know is my heart felt so full of love and pride, seeing you standing up there and telling them you are gay."

Tosh grasped his hand. "I want us to go out together, for dinner one night this week. I want us to hold hands in public like this. I want people to see you and I are in a relationship. There will be people who'll make disparaging comments because I'm with you less than eighteen months after Harry's death, but he wouldn't have been one of them. Are you ready?"

Sam stared ahead for a moment. Was he? Was he ready to not only come out but declare to the world there was a man in his life?

He turned to face Tosh and clutched his other hand. "Are you sure, Tosh? We could maybe ask Darach and Brice to come with us, or Gus and Mel."

"No, I want this to be you and me, out on a date, just the two of us. We could go to the Lodge."

"It's odd. Even though the place has been there for years,

I've never been, just seen it in the magazines."

"I'm going to book us in there, then. It has a great reputation. I deliver the post as well. The owner, Zac McKenzie, is building a house in the grounds for himself and his partner, Seth. You'd like them both. Say you'll come with me."

Their relationship would come out soon, so maybe it was better if they decided when. "Yes, I'd love to come out on a date with you, kind sir, especially if you wear the three-piece suit you have hidden at the back of your wardrobe. I saw it when I was searching for something to put on."

"It's the suit I was married in, but yes, it could do with an airing."

"Shit! Sorry." Sam stared down at his hands.

"No, I looked good in it. I loved him, and I love you." Tosh leaned forward and kissed him gently on the mouth.

"Urgh! Tosh and Sam, sitting in a tree — K. I. S. S. I. N. G. We can't leave you alone for a moment."

Sam pulled back to see Stuart standing in the doorway.

"I've been sent to fetch you. Mum and Dad are here now, and they want to toast you, or something."

"Ready?" Sam said, standing and taking Tosh's hand. "You're going to be part of the clan now."

"I'm ready. Lead on. Whatever happens, I'll be here for you." Sam leaned in and kissed him.

"You may regret that," he said.

"I don't think so," Tosh replied. He picked up Jenny, who had crawled into the kitchen, followed by Sandie. She giggled when he tickled under her chin, shaking her ginger curls.

Sandie grinned at him. "If you ever fancy babysitting, it appears you have a fan."

Tosh handed her back to her mother and grasped Sam's hand. "I always wanted a big family and now I have one."

Chapter Nineteen

Tosh knocked on the door of the manse and stood back, waiting. He checked his appearance once more in the glass and ran his fingers through his hair. Should he knock again?

The door opened, but Sam turned on his heel without saying anything and hurried back into the depths of the house. Tosh followed him, closing the door behind him and found Sam sitting on the sofa in the main room.

"I had a call from the Moderator. Cormac Campbell has complained and apparently he's organizing a petition to have me removed."

Tosh sat next to Sam. "Did he say anything else?"

"They don't have a problem with me being gay, but the session does have the power to remove me if the congregation has lost confidence in me. They can refuse to accept a minister in a same-sex marriage."

Marriage—there it was. Tosh wasn't sure he could think that far yet. He decided not to comment on the possibility.

"Aren't there laws to protect you?"

"I don't know. The church is different. I don't want you to be pulled into this mess. It could get nasty."

"And there was me thinking religion was supposed to bring people together." Tosh sighed. "So much argument over stupid little differences. That's what I can't stand."

"I don't disagree with you. But living in the real world, we know people use religious belief as a stick to beat others and pick and choose which parts of the Bible they follow. Every religion has its sects and differences, some more than others, which followers are willing to die for. There are parts of the Bible I don't accept in their entirety because they come from a time thousands of years ago."

"I came here tonight to go out to dinner with you. I vowed as a teenager not to hide who I was from anybody, and I'm not going to start now. Sunday, you told the people in church you were gay, and tonight, I intend to take you on a date like everyone else. We are going to have a meal, and talk, and even hold hands if we want. The Lodge is owned by a gay man living with his partner, so I reckon we're safe from the bigots there."

"I used to have pictures of Zac McKenzie on my wall when he played for Glasgow. The good thing about football is that you can get away with fancying the players and having their pictures up. I may have stared at him sometimes."

Tosh put his hand to his mouth. "Oh, my God, you wanked off gazing at him, didn't you? I always preferred rugby myself. Footballers fall over if someone goes anywhere near them, not like rugby players, all beef and brawn, getting down and dirty in the ruck and maul. So will you become a red-faced fan boy if he's there tonight, because this I have to see."

"There's every chance I might embarrass myself."

"I doubt you'd be the first. Come on, I'm suited and booted, ready to go out, not that you've said anything."

Sam leaned in and kissed him. "You look drop-dead gorgeous with a cherry on the top. Will that do?"

Tosh touched his chest. "Be still my giddy heart. I could get overwhelmed with these compliments."

"Am I supposed to flatter you? I thought only women wanted to know how beautiful they are. You always look good to me."

"Flattery will get you everywhere. Now go and get changed, will you, or we're going to be late. You and I will stride into that place and hold hands while being led to our table, and if anyone stares at us, we're going to smile back at them. All right?"

"Yes, Tosh."

* * * *

Twenty minutes later, they stepped out of Tosh's car and strolled across the busy car park to the entrance of the Lodge. A young woman greeted them.

"Hello, my name is Caitlin, how can I help you this evening?" If she'd clocked that they were holding hands, she made no reaction at all.

"We're booked in for dinner tonight under the name of Mackintosh."

Caitlin consulted her list. "Of course, would you like to go straight to your table, or order while you have a drink at the bar?"

"We'll go to the table, please. Are you busy tonight?"

"We've a few people in, but we aren't full." She moved in front of them and led them to the dining room and a table for two situated next to a window overlooking the sea. It was light enough to see the waves rolling in and over the rocks.

"I'll leave you to make up your mind, gentlemen."

"Is the owner around tonight?" Tosh asked with an ill-disguised smirk on his face. "Only my partner here is a big fan." A sharp kick against his ankle wiped the smirk from his face.

Caitlin returned the grin. "He is around tonight, helping in and out of the kitchen. I'll mention it to him."

"Please," Sam protested. "There's no need."

"Mr. McKenzie loves to meet fans, but do beware, he has lots of stories." Tosh followed her gaze to a young man reading a book at the next table opposite a teenage girl, dressed in purple, who was similarly occupied. He nodded at Seth and Abby, Zac's daughter. Seth lifted his head and grinned at Caitlin's words.

"He most certainly does. Sometimes you can't shut him up."

Tosh leaned forward. "This is Seth, Zac's partner, and Abby, his daughter. It's the first time Sam has been here, and he's a fan. Ouch, that hurt."

Sam glared at him. "You're embarrassing me," he said through gritted teeth.

"And here's the man in question," Seth said, nodding toward the door.

Zac McKenzie *was* a handsome man. He made his way across the room, and Tosh wanted to laugh as Sam tried to lower himself under the table.

"Are you ready to order yet, gentlemen?"

Sam mumbled his choices, and Tosh gave his while Zac wrote them down.

"I understand you're a fan," Zac said, obviously unable to keep the chuckle out of his voice.

"I saw you play for Scotland several times."

"Would you like an autograph? Or I have signed photographs if you'd prefer."

Tosh grinned. "Oh, I'm sure he'd love a signed photograph, wouldn't you, Sam?"

An older couple appeared at the door. "I'll get you a photograph and sign it for you. Let me sort out this couple first."

"There's no hurry," Sam murmured.

Tosh glanced over at the two men who had arrived. "My turn to fanboy," he said.

"Why, who are they? You always seem to know everyone."

"The joys of being the local postman. The one on the left is John Smith. He's a writer. Writes under the name of Richie MacNeill."

"I've heard of him. He wrote those detective stories they made into a series."

"I have every one of his books. He's also written a movie about his family history due out next year. The other man is his husband, who used to be head teacher of the local primary school. We're too old to have been taught by him. They live along the coast near Portgordon. See, we're not the only gays in the village. If Darach and Brice turn up, or Davy and Jason, we'll have the full set."

"Don't forget Cameron."

"Oh yes, how could I forget Cameron?"

Tosh grabbed Sam's hand. "See, we're not on our own. Whatever happens with the church, we'll cope. You can always get a job somewhere else. There are loads of vacant parishes. I checked."

"But you wouldn't want to leave here, and I don't want to go either. This is our home. When I was in Glasgow, one of the things I discovered about myself was that I missed home. I never expected to."

"Darach was the same. Away for twelve years, and now he wouldn't go back. He's made a home here with Brice."

Caitlin appeared at the table with their starters and placed them on the table. "Scallops for you, sir, and the mussels for you, Reverend. Enjoy your starters."

"These are so fresh," Tosh said, after tucking into his food. "And the bacon tastes like little pieces of heaven. I couldn't be a vegetarian to save my life."

"They get their bacon from the McNaughtons' farm. It said on the back of the menu."

"That would explain it. I don't know how those pigs ever got to market, because Darach's dad loves them so much. Darach used to hate it when he gave the animals names. Maybe Brice will succeed in turning him into a vegetarian after all." He hesitated, trying to decide whether he should ask Sam or not.

"What?" Sam asked. "You've a strange expression on your face. Are the mussels not nice?"

"The mussels are beautiful, and the sauce is to die for. Some might argue I'm being deliberately provocative, defiantly being gay *and* eating sea food."

Sam lifted a scallop on his fork. "I'm doubly guilty as well, then."

Tosh stabbed a mussel with his fork and let the morsel of garlic-flavored loveliness slide down his throat. "No, I was pondering something Darach wanted to tell me, but I didn't want to listen."

"Oh."

The color faded from Sam's face. Tosh glanced around and leaned closer. "You and him? I know something happened between you. Did you ever have feelings for him?"

Shit! "Darach? No, no feelings except maybe shame. He was younger than me. I should have stopped it, but somehow I couldn't." His voice was no more than a whisper. "I don't want you to think badly of me. Do you?"

"Hey, we've all been young and horny and wanted to experiment. I'm not going to ask you for the details. When Darach and I first got together, we were like rabbits and couldn't get enough of each other. I wish my powers of recovery were that good now. I don't blame you. I was in love with him then, but he didn't truly see me until one night when everything changed between us. It didn't stop him going off to university, though. He always wanted to get away from here, and I always wanted to stay — ironic, really. People change. They grow apart. Nothing is guaranteed in this life."

Caitlin appeared and removed the empty plates. The main courses arrived soon after. They ate in silence for a while. Tosh remembered the few occasions he'd come here with Harry. In many ways, Harry and Sam were completely different, but they shared a passionate nature, a desire to help others, and the ability to laugh at themselves when they became too pompous, and both had a tendency to worry too much.

"Are you ready for this meeting?" Tosh asked.

"I don't know. The rules are complicated. As I said, there have been quite a few changes in the church with regard to LGBT issues. If they don't want me to stay on, I'll resign. It's easier."

"You're not going to fight?"

"I want to, but I don't want to be where I'm not wanted. It will break my heart to leave. I love this place with the sea and the mountains behind. I love my churches with their white-washed walls and beautiful stained-glass windows.

169

I love the dark wood of the pulpit here with its carvings, and the simplicity of the communion table with its single candle. When I stand in front of the congregation, I feel at home. Every man or woman can talk directly to God, and I help them find their way to Him. I always liked the way every person is encouraged to have their own relationship with the Almighty."

"Not like how I was brought up," Tosh said.

"No. I think it's why I found it easier to be a minister, and be gay. I reconciled myself to that a long time ago. I didn't feel anything but love when I prayed, and there was no one to step in between me and my faith in God's acceptance to tell me I was wrong. But, if the meeting decides not to move on, then that is their right too. I've prayed God will help them, and me, even if it is for selfish reasons."

Tosh reached out and wrapped his fingers around Sam's hand, not caring who might see, gratified Sam didn't pull away from him. "Whatever happens, you're not alone. When Harry died, you were a good friend to me. You let me find my way out of grief on my own. Darach worried you'd taken advantage of me, but you didn't. You waited until I was ready to move on. I know Harry would approve. Maybe I didn't want to see it at first, but I love you, Sam Carmichael, and if losing Harry taught me anything, it's that you have to grab hold of happiness wherever you find it." Emotion bubbled up within him, threatening to burst like water over a dam. He wiped away a tear and realized Sam was staring at their conjoined hands. A cough disturbed the moment.

"I'll come back when you're ready."

Tosh lifted his gaze to see Zac McKenzie standing with photograph in hand.

Sam pulled away. "No, it's okay. We were just talking. Thank you for bringing me the autograph."

Zac leaned down. "I couldn't help overhearing, I'm sorry. Seth and I heard what happened in the church. News travels fast around here. I hope all goes well at the meeting tomorrow. Maybe one day you'll be allowed to officiate same-sex marriages in church for those who want them. Stranger things have happened."

Tosh thought his heart would melt when Sam smiled and said, "I hope so."

* * * *

A week later, with the meeting scheduled for the next day, they'd had a quiet dinner at Tosh's house. "Stay with me tonight," Tosh said while they washed the dishes.

"I shouldn't. I'm supposed to set a good example about sex before marriage and all that."

"We don't have to have sex," Tosh said, turning on what he hoped was his best puppy-dog expression.

"You're incorrigible. You know I can't resist those eyes. Maybe a cuddle, then, and sleep. I need to have my faculties working tomorrow, and you, no doubt, have to be up before the crack of dawn."

"And if anything else should happen?"

"Brodie!"

"Come on. Let's go in. The quicker we do, the quicker you'll be in my bed and in my arms."

Sam sighed. "And who could argue against such an offer?"

Chapter Twenty

Sam groaned when the alarm sounded at four-thirty the next morning with Tosh's impressive erection pressing against his arse. He stayed put when Tosh kissed his neck and ran his fingers down his chest.

"Too early," he murmured. He didn't want to tell Tosh he'd lain awake for hours listening to him breathing and trying to work out what he was going to say. If he were honest, there wasn't anything to say. It wasn't his job to defend himself. His church had accepted gay ministers a while ago, but his lack of openness would now count against him. He depended on other people wanting him to stay, and he wasn't sure which way the meeting would decide. Even if he got support, the members of the congregation could leave and that would count against him. Daisy McPherson had hinted the petition had gained very few signatures. No doubt Cormac Campbell would present it today.

"I've got to get up," Tosh whispered in his ear. "I don't want to leave you."

"Go on or people will complain their post is late."

Tosh's voice, singing away in the shower, could be heard above the water. Sam wasn't averse to mornings, but if his life moved ahead the way he wanted, he'd have to get used to this. He was enough of a traditionalist not to want to live in sin. At least Tosh believed in marriage, but whether he was ready again was another matter.

The singing and water sounds stopped, and he opened his eyes to witness Tosh coming back into the bedroom with a towel slung around his waist.

"So you didn't jump out of bed and rush downstairs

to make my breakfast, then?" Tosh asked while he dried himself.

Sam gulped. Was he supposed to? Had Harry done the same for Tosh?

Tosh laughed and pointed. "Your face. Don't worry, I don't eat until I get to work, and I usually grab something more substantial at Maggie's café on my round. At least it's fine this morning."

Once dressed, Tosh crossed the room and knelt next to the bed. "I wish I could be there for you this morning. I'll be thinking about you, so ring me when you know anything. They would be stupid to lose you. The place used to be full of old people ready for death, and now you have the youth club, and the school visits, and younger people attending. You've made the church a bigger part of the community. Look at how many people came to the open air service at Easter, down at the harbor, despite the cold."

Tosh kissed him, and Sam longed to drag him back into bed and crush their bodies together in an effort to put off what was to happen later.

Tosh stroked his face. "Your beard could do with a trim. You don't want to appear too much like an Old Testament prophet, or maybe you do."

"I intend on going in there and looking the part," Sam said. "Not just the shirt and collar, but robes and all. You'd better get on."

They held hands until their fingers parted and Tosh pulled away. His footsteps echoed down the wooden stairs and, a few minutes later, the door closed with a click and Sam was left on his own in the gloom of an autumnal morning. He reached over to the alarm clock and reset it for seven, unsure of whether he'd be able to get back to sleep.

No one was more surprised than him to be woken by the Breakfast Show blasting out a loud, indiscriminate tune. After washing and dressing, he sat at Tosh's kitchen table, drinking a large mug of tea and trying to swallow small pieces of toast he'd chewed many times as he thought about the arguments, both theological and moral, he could use to counter at least those of Cormac Campbell. Yes, the Bible did afford him wiggle room, but it wouldn't be enough in the face of major opposition. His hand shook as he picked up and ripped another bite out of the toast. Maggie did bake beautiful bread.

He opened his laptop and read through the information he'd discovered regarding recent LGBT rulings in the church.

A little while later, he climbed into his car and drove the short distance to his house, collected his robe, then drove on to the church on the hill. For a while, he walked around the small courtyard, and, despite the rather biting wind, sat on a bench and stared out at the waves. Overhead, gulls swooped over the sea. Suddenly, a body emerged from the waves followed by another and another, until he noted five dolphins throwing themselves out of the water with sheer joy. For ten minutes, they entertained him, leaping and twisting in the wind and waves until they disappeared once more out of sight.

Before venturing into the church, he checked his phone, noting the many messages from both his family and others. Inside, the church was quiet as it was still early. They were using the room at the back for the meeting. He expected the elders to attend. The group wasn't huge, but their decisions mattered. Elders, once chosen, were elders for life. They took their responsibilities seriously.

Sam sat in the second pew and leaned against the one in front, bowing his head into his hands. He hoped God would be listening and His answer would be yes. He'd said before that maybe it wasn't that God wasn't listening, but that sometimes, like any good parent, he had to say no or not now to requests. Sam stayed there for a while. Only the creak of the door brought him back to the situation at hand.

"I thought you'd be here already, Reverend." Mrs. McPherson stood in the aisle next to the pew.

"I wanted time to myself, to talk."

"I'll leave you to it, Sam, and I'll go and organize tea to go with this shortbread."

It was the first time she'd ever called him by name since he'd become the minister. "Thank you. I don't know what the church would do without you," he said.

She placed a cool hand on his arm. "And without you, this place and my little church would still be full of us old things with yet another congregation dwindled to nothing. Believing there's a higher purpose to anything isn't always easy. Islam says God doesn't send you anything you can't deal with, and maybe that's right. Don't ever think you're alone. There are people who love you, no matter who, or what, you are."

After a few minutes, voices drifted from the back room. Mrs. McPherson had left the door slightly ajar when she'd gone. The time of the meeting was set for eleven, which, glancing at his watch, he realized was fifteen minutes from now. Quite often, he chaired the regular sessions, but this time his only role was to answer questions. He wasn't even sure if he should plead to keep his job, and had agreed to leave the group to debate the future. At least he was certain of Mrs. McPherson's support. Once again, trying to find her son crossed his mind. Offering up a final prayer, Sam edged out of the pew and trudged the distance to the door. After pushing it open, he counted the faces. The Moderator had been called away so had appointed another local minister in his place. Sam was pleased to see his friend, in the seat at the head of the table. He knew the Reverend Duncan Murdoch from the next parish shared his views. Most of the others had arrived. Mary Urquhart, an elder from Duncan's church, had writing paper set out in front of her to take the minutes, and Mrs. McPherson had placed the shortbread and two large teapots in the center. The back door swung open and Cormac Campbell entered with Iain Mackay, another elder, behind him. Also seated was Linda Jameson, from the local medical practice, and Douglas Macduff, a local gardener who took care of many of the church graveyards. With them sat another minister and elder he knew from Presbytery meetings and had no idea how they might vote. These men and women could decide his future, although the congregation could still affect proceedings.

"Everyone here? Good. Let's get this over with, shall we?" Duncan Murdoch announced. "It's far too nice a day to be stuck in here."

Campbell stared at Sam, his eyes blazing. "I have a petition I'd like to submit to the meeting." He handed to paper to the chair. "I'd hoped the Moderator would be here. As you can see, there are people who agree with me about Mr. Carmichael's fitness to serve."

Sam took a seat as far away from Campbell as possible and said nothing. Mrs. McPherson poured mugs of tea for them and took her seat to the side of him. Sam held his mug in the hope it might steady his fraying nerves.

Duncan Murdoch shuffled the papers in front of him. "Thank you, Mary. If you'll take the minutes, we'll begin. We are here to decide what to do about Reverend Carmichael's recent statement, and whether we want him to continue in this parish."

Sam smiled at Duncan's deliberate use of his title. It was clear what his views would be.

"The Bible calls homosexuality an abomination. I'm sure we can agree on that fact," Campbell began.

Daisy McPherson immediately straightened in her seat. "I think you'll find there are several interpretations of various verses in both Testaments, not to mention a lot of other so-called rules which no one follows today. After all, Cormac, your father made a living fishing for shellfish and the like."

"Daisy has a point, Cormac. I'm not sure we'll get anywhere if we start throwing Bible quotes at each other. Every one of us knows our Bible, after all."

Sam glanced at Linda Jameson, medical practice manager and mother of three. She was one of the newer elders, thoroughly efficient and organized. Suffering fools was not within her remit.

Cormac's face now burned red with fury. "But surely the Bible has to be the basis for this discussion. Whatever the Moderator may declare, homosexuality is wrong, and I want no part of it in my kirk. Nothing you say will persuade me otherwise, and I'm sure Iain agrees with me."

Next to him, Iain Mackay nodded. He and Cormac had been friends since childhood so Sam hadn't expected anything different.

"This parish would have died if the Reverend Carmichael hadn't come back home. He achieved a first at Glasgow and has a great record of working with both old and young. This area was lucky to get him before an urban parish snapped him up," Linda continued.

"He should have told us then, and allowed us to make the decision," Cormac protested.

"How could he? The synod hadn't said anything then. Times have changed recently, and the Church of Scotland has always led the way. We had women ministers long before England."

"Linda's right there, Cormac. You can't argue with that." Daisy McPherson crossed her arms.

Cormac harrumphed, making his views clear.

Linda tutted. "Typical. I expect you'd prefer women stuck at home still. Well, we're not. The reverend has my full support. I've brought my children up to accept others. I don't care what Sam does in his private life because that's exactly what it is — *his* private life."

Cormac sneered. "So you'd be happy to have Brodie Mackintosh, a papist, whispering his blasphemy in our reverend's ear, would you?"

All faces turned to stare at him. Well, Tosh had been right. Sam cleared his throat in an effort to reply.

"Brodie and I are in a relationship. I'm not going to deny that. Brodie was brought up a Catholic, but as you know, he's attended services here. His beliefs are his business, but he also believes in me."

Daisy McPherson patted his hand. "I'm glad," she

said quietly, before turning to the others. "The Reverend Carmichael has my support as well. Some of you knew my husband." She glowered at Cormac Campbell. "He believed a woman should stay at home under his hand. We had a son, Malachi. I have no idea whether he's alive or dead, because when he was eighteen, he told us he was gay and my husband threw him out. I never saw him again. *My* religion puts love first."

"So we're left with four others."

The other minister sided with Sam, while the elder agreed reluctantly with Cormac. That left Mary and Douglas. Cormac folded his arms and glowered once more.

"I want the reverend to stay," Mary replied, holding on to Cormac's intimidating gaze. "I've seen first-hand how the old people with no one else to visit love him when he goes around the homes. Sometimes he'll sit and listen for hours. I've seen him there nearly asleep with tiredness, sitting with someone who has no one else while they died."

Cormac thumped the table. "Typical females, the lot of you thinking with your emotions."

Rising from his seat, Douglas Macduff knocked back his chair and hurried out of the room and into the main part of the church. The others glanced at each other.

Cormac shrugged. "What's up with him? He's always been odd. Cycling everywhere and not eating meat, working for the local council. He never goes out for a drink and lives alone. No woman would have him, I suppose."

Sam hadn't ever paid much attention to Douglas. Sometimes Sam would catch him staring in his direction with a wistful expression on his face as he tended the graves and cut the grass. Had there been more to that look? Should he get up and find the man, or would it appear as though he was trying to unduly influence him?

Daisy rose from her seat and peeked around the door before returning and filling the teapot with hot water from the boiler. "Give him a while. He's praying. This is a matter of religion, after all. He has a right to ask for guidance. Let's have more tea and biscuits."

For twenty minutes they sat in awkward silence. Sam thanked Mrs. McPherson for the refreshments. Should he leave?

"I'm sorry. I needed to think." Douglas emerged through the door once more and sat at the table. "I'd like to hear what the reverend has to say before I make my decision."

"He said more than enough as far as I'm concerned. What else could he have to say?"

"I don't know, Mr. Campbell, but I want to hear it anyway. I'm an elder as well. We're all here to serve his congregation as well as God."

Sam couldn't help wondering if Douglas' knees were knocking under the table as he folded his arms and stuck out his chin. He'd never seen the usually quiet man so determined and realized he needed to think carefully before he spoke.

"When I first decided to train to be a minister, many people, including my family, were shocked. I don't come from a religious background and my family aren't churchgoers, but I was called to service and acted upon that call. When I'd finished my training, I was offered several inner city parishes, but my one thought was to come home. I love this church. All I've ever wanted to do is serve God and my congregation with honesty and humility. I've always known about my sexuality but chose to keep the information to myself."

"What made you change your mind?" Douglas asked.

"A few things. I listened to young people being brave enough to live their lives in the open. I heard stories of what had happened in the past. The Synod voted to allow gay ministers and even married gay ministers in time, and…" Should he say it out loud? He picked up the mug of tea and swallowed a large mouthful. "And I fell in love and didn't want to hide. I believe God made me as I am for a purpose. That's it, really. I want to stay here and serve, if you'll have me."

"Then I vote to let you stay. Times change. Reverend Carmichael has my vote."

"That means the vote is five to three, and my vote would make no difference." Sam thought Duncan looked happy not to have to give an opinion.

Cormac thumped the table, making them jump. "This doesn't end here. The congregation may have other ideas and vote with their feet, but I intend take my complaint further than the local presbytery. I shan't be attending in future."

"Good riddance."

Sam stared at Linda. "I'm sorry, Reverend. I shouldn't have said that out loud."

"I'm not staying here to be insulted by a chit of a girl. We're leaving."

Iain Mackay followed Cormac across the room then slammed the door behind them. Relieved at their abrupt departure, Sam sighed loudly. "Thank you," he said simply. "But he's still right. There will be others who aren't happy to have a gay minister, especially one in a relationship."

Mary smiled at him. "I know I've made the right choice. People love you, Sam, and those who have a problem will come round. They know you and that makes a difference. You're not an outsider imposed on them. You're one of us, a local lad who came home to serve. It's good for us to be challenged and shaken up. I'll get the minutes typed up. Can I give you a lift, Linda?"

Duncan Murdoch held out his hand. Sam clasped it, wanting really to pull the man into a hug. "Good. I'll let the powers that be know the decision. The petition didn't get much support. I think you owe Daisy here thanks for that, from what I've heard."

Sam nodded, unable to speak, knowing how close he was to crying. He bid goodbye to the others until only Daisy and Douglas remained.

So far Douglas hadn't said anything more. Sam had the feeling he wanted to talk. Daisy McPherson put her hand on his arm. "Give us a minute."

Sam nodded. "I'll ring Tosh. He'll be on his round and going mad by now. I'll be through there."

* * * *

When he returned twenty minutes later, the old lady was sitting on her own. "I expect Tosh was pleased at your news."

"He was, and my parents. Douglas has gone, then?"

"He has. He and my son were close when they were young. I'd always wondered about them. I'm won't say anything more, except it's so sad. I hope you and Tosh are happy together. Love is love, after all."

She wrapped her arms around him, and he did the same to her, more determined than ever to try to find the son she'd been forced to give up.

"I'll leave you to it," she said. "I'm sure you have things to do."

Sam returned to the same pew he'd sat in earlier. It wasn't over yet. When someone came out, even as publicly as he'd done, they still needed to do it time and time again. He stared up at the ceiling. Now he didn't have to live a lie. Despite his status, he and Tosh had a future together, and they'd work out any problems because they had the will to do so. Sam bowed his head and offered up a silent thanks before making his way to the front door and locking it behind him.

"I wondered whether to come in or not."

Sam turned on the top step. There, with his bike leaning against the wall, stood Tosh, in his uniform, grinning from ear to ear.

"The post will be late."

Tosh walked slowly toward him, taking the steps one at a time until he reached the top. "Maybe a little, but I couldn't wait to see you."

"You know this isn't the end, don't you? There'll still be

voices in the congregation who'll complain, and Campbell won't give up so easily."

Tosh placed a hand on his cheek, and Sam glanced around, concerned who might witness this public display of affection.

"It doesn't matter. You've done so much for these people. You've worked selflessly, day and night, giving your love wherever it was needed, and now I want some of it. I know I can't have it all."

The space between them closed as Tosh wrapped his arms around Sam's back and pulled him in for a kiss. Sam didn't fight it, despite his fears. The kiss was warm, but brief, and truthfully, Sam wanted more.

"You do realize we're on the steps of my church where anyone could see."

Tosh laughed. "Let them look. We've nothing to hide now, and if I'm going to be a minister's husband..."

Sam's heart fluttered and his throat dried. "You want to. I mean I wanted to ask you, but I wasn't sure if it was too soon. We couldn't just live together. I have to set an example to others, you know."

"That may not be the most exciting proposal."

"I'm sorry. Should I get down on one knee? I don't have a ring."

"There's a lot to consider," Tosh said, smiling.

"And you have your round to finish."

"I do, and you're interfering with the delivery of the Royal Mail, which is a criminal offence, but I should be home by two, if you're not busy."

"I may be able to squeeze you in."

Tosh moved down one step. "Oh, I hope so. I'll be waiting for you, usual place."

Sam's eyes widened as Tosh cupped his crotch, and his cock stirred. "Stop it, I've the old folk's home to visit now, and I can't go there with a raging...you know what, can I?"

Tosh hurried down the rest of the steps and picked up his bike, then blew Sam a kiss. "I'll be waiting," he said.

Sam straightened his clothes absentmindedly as heat rushed into his cheeks and elsewhere, before double-checking he'd locked the door. Sitting a few minutes later in his car, gazing at his church then the view of the sea between the houses, he remembered how mad some of his fellow trainees had thought him for staying home. Now he was sure it was the best decision he'd ever made.

Epilogue

December, a few months later

Sam stared at the ring on his finger with a huge grin on his face. "Do you think they'll forgive us for not inviting everyone?"

Tosh heaved the large suitcase into the living room. "Not in the case of your lot. I need to unpack, and we have matters to organize. I hope we've done the right thing interfering."

Sam wrapped his arms around his husband. "Of that, I'm sure. Without Daisy McPherson, we might not be here now. She fought to keep me and didn't waver, and I've no idea how many people she spoke to behind the scenes. I may have lost a few members of the congregation, but others have started attending. The local MP turning up didn't do any harm either. We've a couple of hours. I asked her to come to the church for afternoon tea rather than here. With a couple of days remaining before Christmas, I'm sure she and the others will have been busy this week decorating and cleaning. Now, let's shower together and wipe off the grime of London's streets."

"Together?" Tosh questioned. "I thought you'd have had enough of me by now."

Sam pulled him in tighter and kissed him. "I will never have had enough of you, Brodie Mackintosh. Last one up the stairs and naked gets on their knees first."

Sam moved more quickly through the door. "You're standing still," he said at the bottom of the stairs.

Tosh grinned. "Maybe I *want* to be on my knees."

Sam didn't have to be told twice and, minutes later, he

stood braced against the wall shouting Tosh's name as he came over Tosh's chest, the water washing away the ropes of white liquid. Sam was careful, despite Tosh's protests that he was in little danger with Sam's viral load being undetectable. They had fun working out different ways to bring each other off, and Sam had made certain Tosh had packed a few glass items for their brief honeymoon.

At three, Sam stood in his church, gazing around. Ostentatious decoration wasn't something the Protestant Church of Scotland encouraged. There were no wall paintings and a minimal amount of stained glass, but the communion table had a nativity scene surrounded by beautiful foliage, and to one side stood a large cross made up of red and white flowers with holly. It was simple but beautiful. The sound of a female voice raised in song drifted through the slightly open door to the back room.

Tosh threaded his arm through Sam's. "I've always loved *In the Bleak Midwinter*. I hope it's warmer through there. Why are churches always cold?"

Sam gazed around. "One, because they're too big, and two, because heat is expensive. I told you to wear a warmer coat. Come on, let's not keep them waiting."

Sam pushed through the door to the back room and found the table set out with sandwiches and Christmas cake.

"I thought you might be hungry after traveling back." Mrs. McPherson greeted Sam by hugging him then stroked his face. "Thank goodness. You've trimmed that ridiculous beard. This is much better. You look years younger."

Over the last few months, she'd become like another grandmother to him and fussed as much as his own did. Despite his worries, his grandmother had taken his relationship with Tosh in her stride.

"So did you do it?" she asked.

Sam held out his hand, and Tosh did the same.

"What beautiful rings." She wiped away a tear. "I'm so pleased for you both."

"And you'll be at the party tomorrow. No telling anyone, though. We're going to announce it to everyone then."

She turned a key shape at her lips. "No one will get anything out of me. Now, it's brass monkeys out there. I made tea, so sit down and get yourselves warmed through."

Sam took a seat, and Daisy positioned herself on a chair, ready to pour the tea.

Sam had planned his words carefully. "While we were in London, we met someone." He nodded to Tosh, who disappeared through the door.

"We know it's been years, but after all you did for me, for us, we had to see if we could find your son."

"No." She covered her face with one hand.

"He wanted to see you. So he's traveled back here."

"He's here? Now? Actually here?" Tears streamed down her cheeks

Sam nodded. "We told him everything you told us. He doesn't blame you for what happened."

"And he's okay?"

"I'm more than okay, Mum."

The man who stepped through the door stood six feet tall in his dark coat. His hair, now flecked with gray, lay slicked back, and a hint of tears glistened in his eyes.

Sam and Tosh watched as Mal Pearson, as he was now known, wrapped his arms around his mother and lifted her off her feet.

"You grew up so handsome," she said when he put her down.

"And you're exactly as I remember you."

"With more gray hair, a few more pounds, and arthritis. Oh, Mal, I can't believe they found you. I should have searched myself, but I was too scared. You look so well, and prosperous."

"I am, Mum. It's a long story, but I'm a barrister in London. I'm head of chambers and... I'm getting married in the New Year. He's here as well."

"Oh my, I can't... All this... So much to take in." She

turned to Sam and Tosh, tears pouring down her face. "Thank you so much. I need to pinch myself." She grasped her son's hand. "You *are* staying for a while, aren't you?"

Sam wiped his eyes and stepped forward. "Why don't you take Daisy to your hotel and come to the party tomorrow? It's at the local community center. Daisy will know the way."

Daisy crossed the floor and clung to Sam like a limpet. "I can't tell you what this means to me."

"Come on, Mum. We've such a lot to discuss."

Sam took Tosh's hand as mother and son left together. "It's moments like this which make everything worthwhile. Now, I'm starving. Let's eat these lovely sandwiches and enjoy the rest of the day before tomorrow's excitement."

* * * *

"Come on, we have things to do." Sam sat on the edge of their bed. He liked thinking of it as *their* bed and not simply his bed, in their bedroom, and their house.

"Aw, come back to bed. How often do I get a lie-in?" Tosh pulled back the duvet, revealing his erect cock surrounded by dark hair. Sam couldn't help licking his lips.

"You are a bad man, Brodie Mackintosh." Sam leaned over and licked the bead of clear liquid from the swollen head.

"Suck me."

"You're sure?"

Tosh placed a finger on Sam's lips. "We've discussed this until the cows come home. Now, I want to feel your mouth on my cock. I don't think it'll take much time. I did give it a few strokes of encouragement while you were in the shower."

Sam enclosed the head in his mouth and sucked while Tosh squirmed and gasped under him. He loved being able to tease Tosh to his climax and the taste of him as he swallowed him down. He wrapped a hand around the base

187

and stroked. Tosh stiffened under his touch and thrust.

"Yes, that's it. Oh, God, don't stop."

Salty liquid flooded into Sam's mouth and he swallowed until Tosh was spent. He ignored his own needs and lay beside his husband.

"Told you it wouldn't take long," Tosh gasped between pants.

"I still worry," Sam said.

"I know you do, but the risks are tiny, and when we're ready for more, we'll go at it like bunnies. There aren't any rules, Sam, about what we should do in bed. Only we decide when, and we decide together. Anyway, you give great blow jobs. And talking of blow jobs, now it's your turn."

A little while later, Sam dropped the condom into the bin.

Tosh sat up. "And now we'd better get a move on. We're going to be behind with you keeping me in here too long."

Sam rolled on top of Tosh and kissed his face and mouth then along his jaw before sucking on his earlobe. "For that, you're going to butter every single one of those sandwiches."

Tosh grinned up at him. "Nah, Maggie will be here in forty minutes. I got mate's rates on a whole range of stuff. Everything is ordered."

"But I thought you said you'd put loaves in the chest freezer."

Tosh chuckled. "Sorry, Reverend, I may have told a little white lie. This is my treat, but we'd better get going or Maggie and Mel will catch us in our smalls."

By one in the afternoon, the dining room table was laden with all manner of buffet food and bottles of champagne. Sam and Tosh had dressed, had had breakfast and were glad to see the weather two days before Christmas was cold and crisp with the sky a glorious shade of blue.

In small groups, people began to arrive. Tosh's mother and father were first, followed by Daisy McPherson and her son with his partner. She was full of their wedding plans, and Sam had never seen her so happy. The Carmichaels drifted in, and the level of noise increased. Darach and Brice appeared behind them, having come through the French doors at the rear of the house. Cameron came straight from school. Photographs were taken of the five Carmichael brothers, the first time they'd been together for months, as Hamish was staying for Christmas. When all the guests were there, and people were demanding food, Sam poured a drink for everyone and stood next to Tosh in front of the French doors to the garden. He held Tosh's hand.

"It is so good to have everyone here. The last few months have been tough for both of us. It's not everyone who would take on a man like me who had hidden himself from everyone, and support me without question in my job. Now that everything is behind us, we wanted to get everyone together to make an announcement."

"I hope he's making an honest man of you," Sam's dad shouted.

Sam cleared his throat. "Ah, well, that particular horse has already bolted. We got married last week in Glasgow. We hope you don't mind. We didn't want any fuss, and we wanted to be married when we moved in here together."

"You sneaky bastards," Stuart cried. "Still, means we didn't have to buy you a present." Aisling punched his arm.

"We don't need anything. If you want to spend your money, make a donation to a charity of your choice."

Alec stepped forward and held up his glass of champagne. "Well, as the eldest, I'm going to make the toast. To my brother, Sam, and the man brave enough to take him on. To Sam and Tosh."

Everyone raised their glasses. Backs were slapped and the rings examined. There was laughter and smiles and too much eating and drinking, followed by ill-advised singing and dancing.

After watching their parents twirl each other around the floor, Sam proffered his hand to his husband. How good it was to be able to use that word. "Care to dance?" he said.

Tosh leaned his head on Sam's shoulder while Sam

wrapped his arms around Tosh and pulled him close. "This has been great. I love having everyone here with us. You've made me such a happy man, Tosh."

Tosh lifted his head and kissed him. "After Harry, I never thought I'd be happy again, but you made me see I could be, even if I'm now part of this lot. And we've our first Christmas and Hogmanay. I can't wait."

Sam hugged Tosh tighter and twirled him round. "Come on, let's show this lot how to strut their stuff properly, shall we?"

The floor cleared around them as Sam spun Tosh then bent him over his arm with a flourish. To the sound of cheers and clapping, he and Tosh danced on.

Sporting Chance

Excerpt

Chapter One

Oh hell!
His arse hit the ice.
This was going to be so embarrassing.
He really should have looked where he was going and taken more care. It wasn't that he meant to show off in front of the kids when they'd goaded him into demonstrating how he could skate backward. But that was how he found himself crashing into another body, a rather large male body, then scrabbling, unsuccessfully, to try to get himself up as he apologised. Iestyn heard the kids laughing. How the hell was he going to get up and retain some sort of dignity? Whose bloody idea had it been to come on this skating trip from school, and why had he volunteered to go? He heard a voice—a rather gorgeous lyrical voice— say something, but he wasn't sure what. He found himself

looking up into the face of the most handsome man he'd ever seen.

"Would you like some help getting up?" the vision said, holding out a hand.

Iestyn took the help offered and let the good-looking stranger pull him to his feet. He was shocked to find, when he'd stood up, that the man appeared to be significantly taller than his own nearly six feet.

"Thanks," he said, brushing the ice from his trousers. He glanced over to find the kids staring at him. "What? You've seen a man fall over before, haven't you? Even a teacher."

But they just kept on staring at the man who had helped him up.

"Sorry about that lot. Honestly, you can't take them anywhere, and thanks for hauling me up. I'm not very good at this lark, really." He didn't want to stare but he couldn't resist looking the man up and down. His rescuer was impressively built with blue eyes and blond hair that seemed determined to defy any sort of styling.

"Yeah, that much is obvious but don't worry. I can cope with men falling at my feet. I get it a lot, though usually it's because they've just missed tackling me. The blond, godlike creature held out his hand. "Sorry. It's not often that I have to introduce myself. My name is Dan Morgan."

"Ah, judging from the reaction of the kids, I should have heard of you."

A smaller man, who was standing behind them, sniggered at his comment.

One of the boys rushed forward. "Can I have your autograph, Dan?" he asked.

The other kids came forward too, offering whatever they could find for him to sign.

"You don't have any idea who I am, do you?" the younger man said as he signed the autographs.

"No, sorry. I don't, but obviously the kids do, so you're either some sort of pop star or, from what you've said, a sportsman. I'm guessing rugby."

Josh, a character in Iestyn's form, stepped forward. "Take no notice of Mr Jones. The only game he plays is chess. He wouldn't know one end of a rugby ball from the other."

"Well, to be fair, they are actually pretty similar," Dan replied.

Iestyn frowned at Josh, not for the first time, then looked back at Dan. "So you play rugby then, and I should know this because?"

"Bloody hell, sir. Sorry, but he's Dan Morgan." Now it was Josh's turn to frown. "He plays for Glamorgan Giants and Wales. Most experts reckon that he's going to be Welsh captain for the Six Nations. Call yourself Welsh, sir!"

"Actually, that's rather a moot point. I may be called Jones but I wasn't born in Wales, despite my father's best efforts. I was born in the Highlands of Scotland, because we were on holiday and I came earlier than expected. My dad was gutted, I can tell you."

"Sounds like an interesting story," Dan said. "Perhaps you'd like to tell it to me sometime soon, maybe over dinner."

Iestyn Jones blinked a few times and wondered if he'd heard right. Had this guy just asked him out? Dan had to be at least ten years younger than him, not to mention six inches taller.

Dan passed him a card that said "Ring me" and gave a number. He smiled and walked back to greet his friend who had been standing some distance away. Watching him go, Iestyn held onto the card and twirled it in his fingers, not sure how to react to this strange development.

"You're in there, sir," he heard a familiar voice say.

"Shut up, Josh. Come on. I see Miss Jenkins over there tapping her watch. It's time we weren't here."

"But, sir, he's gay and you're gay," Josh persisted.

"Really?" He shouldn't have been surprised. His gaydar was normally useless. "Never mind that. I don't need a matchmaker, thank you." That he was gay was no secret to the kids or to any of the other staff.

His best friend Julie Jenkins came towards him. "Is it right what the kids have just told me? Have you just been asked out by Dan Morgan? My God, he's gorgeous. I can't tell you how many women would like a piece of him."

"Well," Iestyn said, grinning widely. "It seems that Dan Morgan wants a piece of me."

* * * *

"So are you going to ring him, then?" Julie asked that night.

Julie was Iestyn's oldest friend. They'd lived on the same street and gone to the same schools. However, their choice of university had parted them and Julie had gone off and got married. It had lasted all of three years before she had returned home. Now Julie taught music at two schools on a part-time basis.

It was Friday, so tradition had it that their group went out, had a few drinks, then went to one home or another for takeaway curry, pizza, or Chinese. There were six of them in their little group — Iestyn and Julie, along with Matt who taught PE, Sian who taught art, and Gareth, who had claimed to teach science — however, not everyone had been convinced of that. He'd since trained as a plumber, having found that teaching was not for him. These days they were lucky to get him out on a Friday as 'time was money'. Still, it was nice to have a tame plumber on call.

Lastly, there was Kate, who taught a variety of subjects that ended in 'ology'. Most people who saw them all together assumed that they were three couples, which wasn't the case.

Except for Julie, they had all started teaching at the school at the same time and had become friends. As they were all sad and single, as Gareth often described them, they had developed the habit of going out on Friday nights. Of course, nothing was ever that simple about the group dynamic. Julie fancied Matt, who was completely oblivious – or appeared to be. Sian fancied Kate but said nothing. Iestyn thought both the other men were handsome but as both appeared to be straight – other than the occasional drunken snog – he kept on looking elsewhere. Now he had Dan's phone number.

As soon as he'd got home that night, he'd Googled Dan Morgan. Iestyn had to admit that the guy looked great in shorts. Those thighs and shoulders were impressive, and he even looked good in a suit. There were several photos of him receiving prizes for being the young Welsh player of the year. The stories mentioned Dan's apparently now ex-boyfriend Aron Roberts. Iestyn noted that they'd been together since high school, but there was no official announcement of why they were no longer a couple.

He disliked uncertainties and he wasn't about to step on anyone's toes. He knew he was an old-fashioned romantic but he didn't like to share and he'd never really been into one-night stands. Well, not often, especially after the embarrassing incident in the bus shelter all those years ago. He'd managed to get to the age of thirty-four and had slept with fewer than ten people, although 'slept with' was pushing it for some of them. He'd had two long-term boyfriends but no one else since he'd had his heart broken by Steve.

He couldn't understand why the handsome rugby international star should have given him his phone number.

"Are you ever going to answer me, or are you already imagining what he could be doing with you?" Julie continued.

"Sorry," Iestyn replied. "I was just thinking."

"Yeah, we can imagine," Gareth commented. "He's a big lad. Are you sure you can handle him?" He laughed at his own innuendo.

"God, he wishes," Matt added. "He really is a fantastic player and he should be Welsh captain soon. Some people think he might be made captain for the Six Nations. Hey, if you get to shag him, d'you think you could get him to come to the school to talk to my boys? A local lad who made good always helps inspire them."

"Hmm, I haven't even decided if I'm going to ring him yet. From what I've read, he had a long-term boyfriend. They could get back together again. Perhaps this Dan is trying to make him jealous, and I'm not that sort of bloke."

"Looked him up, then," Sian said, smiling.

"Well, yeah, it's not every day that a bloke ten years younger and six inches taller, with more than enough muscles to spare and a great arse, gives you his number. I'm knackered, not bloody dead. Well, not quite."

"Him and his boyfriend split up a while back, according to the gossip columns," Sian continued. "The boyfriend went to America to work and there's no rugby there so..."

"Therefore, I repeat my question," said Julie. "Are you going to ring him? He obviously wants you to. Otherwise, he wouldn't have given you his number."

"But why would he give Iestyn his number? Sorry, I know you're my friend, but let's face it—you're a nerd and a geek. You're hardly love's young dream, are you?" Gareth, as always, said what others just thought. "And the man is fit. Whereas you consider table tennis to be active. I don't get it. What could he possibly have in common with you?"

"Yeah, I suppose you've got the advantage of height, but you're out of condition and you could do with losing a few pounds," Matt added.

"Not to mention your hair is beginning to recede and you're as blind as a bat without those glasses. Why you don't wear contacts, I don't know," Julie finished.

"Okay, anything else before I go home and put a bag over my head? So far I'm fat, geeky and myopic, but I am six foot so that makes up for it."

"Actually, you do scrub up well, when you try. I'll give you some exercises that'll tone you up. Perhaps you can start coming to the gym with me. Tell you what, why don't you join me tomorrow?" Matt said.

"Suddenly, I'm really hungry. Think we can forgo the karaoke tonight? So what are we having and where are we going to eat?" Iestyn said.

"It's my turn," Kate replied. "So let's have Chinese and pick up some more to drink. You'll have something to work off in the morning, then."

"Sounds good to me. Chinese is always better when there are lots of us as we can eat each other's. Drink up and we can get going."

More books from
Alexa Milne

What would you give up for love?

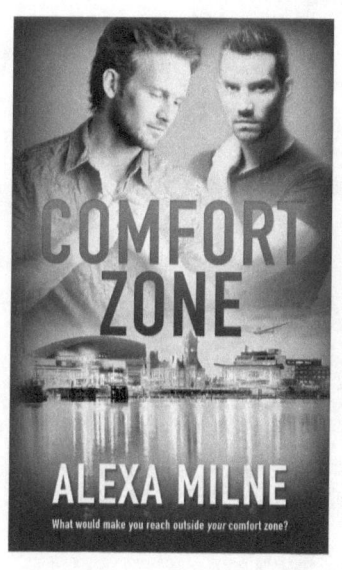

What would make you reach outside your comfort zone?

Sometimes you only need to believe.

An act of kindness is never wasted.

About the Author

Alexa Milne

Originally from South Wales, Alexa has lived for over thirty years in the North West of England. Now retired, after a long career in teaching, she devotes her time to her obsessions.

Alexa began writing when her favourite character was killed in her favourite show. After producing a lot of fanfiction she ventured into original writing.

She is currently owned by a mad cat and spends her time writing about the men in her head, watching her favourite television programmes and usually crying over her favourite football team.

Alexa Milne loves to hear from readers. You can find contact information, website details and an author profile page at https://www.pride-publishing.com/

www.ingramcontent.com/pod-product-compliance
Lightning Source LLC
Chambersburg PA
CBHW020431180626
46812CB00003B/1173